# OMEGA CHATTEL

## *The Omega Misfits #5*

### by

### Wendy Rathbone

Omega Chattel: The Omega Misfits Book 5
Copyright © August 2020 by Wendy Rathbone and Eye Scry
Publications.

www.eyescrypublications.com

ISBN: 978-1-942415-36-7
TITLE: Omega Chattel: The Omega Misfits Book 5
Author: Wendy Rathbone
Cover by: Wendy Rathbone

Address all inquiries to the author at:
wrathbone@juno.com

*For Della, as always...*

Special thanks to my amazing beta reader, the talented Jackie North, who accommodates me when I have rushed deadlines and never complains about it.

# Chapter One

*Alli*

A river of lights cascaded across the Alpha's body.

Here in the Trenches—which was what the street boys called the gutters of deep Old Town where they worked—the neon never stopped. In the daylight it became visible only in the dark shop windows of establishments like bars, tattoo shops, and massage parlors. But at night the multi-colored signs promising dark distractions sent their quasar-streams across the broken sidewalks and oil-stained asphalt of a world made prettier only by the misty dreams of escaping it.

I was sort of following the Alpha. Sort of. I had my reasons.

Number one: He looked like he had money. Looks were never a guarantee, though this one was handsome, but I had to start somewhere for the night, right?

Number two: He didn't seem to be sexually interested in the Omega boys peddling themselves on every corner. Most Alphas who came down here wanted that. Or drugs. So maybe, just maybe that meant he'd be less creepy than the fat, older Alphas I'd seen picking up the corner boys and driving them away.

Number three: I was tired and hungry after three nights out. He looked big and strong, not someone I'd have to work hard at to get him going if that's what he might want. He'd dominate for sure. He'd take. He'd pay—hopefully. I'd never done this before, so what did I know? Afterward, maybe I could afford a burger and a room for the night.

Number four: He smelled like an autumn night when the world is growing colder and the air takes on a pale orange sheen and maybe in the distance you can feel a storm coming, electric, ionizing the air, giving you a feeling of stunned existence. He had the kind of essence that made your soul turn over hard causing the entire universe to tremble for a moment. Yeah. He smelled like that.

I couldn't resist it.

I'd been on the streets only three days, sleeping in the alcove of a dilapidated warehouse along an alley inhabited by overflowing dumpsters, crushed and stained cardboard boxes and, scurrying through the garbage, the occasional rustle of an antique wind, or a rat. I'd gone through all the water I'd brought in my backpack, as well as the few nutri-bars I'd managed to steal from Zilly's kitchens the day before I ran away from the chattel farm.

The conditions here were fucked. I granted that. No argument. And I'd been kind of stupid. Okay, *and* rash. I hadn't made any plans. I figured things would get tougher before they got easier. But I didn't care when I ran. I needed to be away from that farm. Far away. I needed to save myself.

My Omega house dad, Gray, who oversaw Section Four of the farm where I grew up, had been a royal pain in my ass since I could remember. Gods, I hated him; he was such a pervy moron! He said such stupid things all the time and would never allow any boy to correct him—called it arguing. He never let us do stuff like the other house dads did in the other Sections. We never got to stay up late, or have extra desserts, or a day off from homework, or anything else. He was never lenient. And he had this thing about coming into our rooms at night and just standing there watching us sleep. I knew this because I would pretend to be asleep but open my eyes just a crack, and there he'd be, silent and watching. Ugh. So gross!

If Gray ever caught any of us doing anything with each other, even just a kiss, he'd smack the shit out of us, then lock us in a closet. Worse, if he caught Omega boys fucking, which of course was forbidden but hell, what did he expect?—we only had each other—he'd make them strip in front of everyone, then force them to wear a special belt that had ties that attached to your dick and forced it back toward your balls. This contraption had a space for the balls, too, keeping them pulled back, and the cords went up over the ass and attached to the belt. He'd fasten that weird belt really tight until kids actually screamed. Then he'd throw them in a closet for a day wearing only that, and they'd have no food or water, either.

How do I know about this? It happened to me a dozen times. Along with more smacks than I could count accompanied by words to the effect of: "You're no better than a piece of shit scraped off a shoe. Remember that."

I got in trouble a lot for giving him what he called "sassy looks." Sometimes I got in trouble for nothing I could figure. I came to believe he simply hated me.

Regarding the punishments for sex, well, I was still a virgin. I never actually fucked my Omega brothers. I just liked to cuddle with them when I was littler. But Gray didn't care. He'd find us sleeping in the same bed and he'd punish us as if we were the filthiest creatures on the planet.

Cade, my best friend at the farm, brought the abuse to the warden's attention a couple of times, only to be ignored. Patted on the head. Set aside.

House-dad Gray hated me so much he'd make up reasons for me to go into that closet. Several times he would join me and pinch me all over my naked body, including on my balls, really hard until I cried. He would accuse me of fraternizing, which I honestly never did.

He would say, "You are a very bad boy. This will teach you not to think with your dick."

When I got older, and bolder, I'd argue, figuring things couldn't get worse. I'd say to him, "You're the one with dick on the mind all the time."

Yeah, that got him really mad and he'd go a bit rougher on me, leaving marks, telling me I would amount to nothing and he'd make sure the warden knew I was not fit for the mating halls when I turned eighteen, repeating that I was worth only doing menial labor jobs around the farm.

Then one day I saw him with a younger Omega. I didn't know him well, but I knew his name. Sai was about fifteen, and Gray shoved him into a closet while the boy cried and cried.

The door got left a little ajar and I happened to be in the punishment room for yet another infraction, told to sit in a chair and face the wall. Of course I turned my head and saw Gray pinching the boy just like he did me, but he didn't stop there. He shoved the boy against the wall and pulled up his robe.

I witnessed the rape in a sort of dazed state of shock.

When Gray came out of the closet, adjusting his robe, he glanced at me as if he'd forgotten he'd put me in the punishment room against the corner.

I was staring right at him instead of at the wall as instructed. I did not look away like I should have. I did not act innocent and scared and stupid. Not anymore. I was almost eighteen, almost ready for the mating hall to meet my first Alpha in a Burn. Ready to defy Gray's negative reports on me and beg the warden for my right to service Alphas and be subject to menial labor for the rest of my life.

But without thinking of the ramifications, I said to Dad-Gray as he left the weeping boy in the closet, "Fucking bastard."

He merely shrugged and said, "You're on your way to an institution, Alli. No one will have you after I make my report to the warden about how unfit you are. And about how you're not even a real virgin."

"I am a virgin!"

"I'm sure I don't believe you for one second. But we can make sure you're not when I'm done with you." He indicated the closet where his most recent victim remained, the sounds of his quiet whimpering muffled by the now closed door.

The air had gone terribly still. I let out a hiss. "You're the one who should be in an institution."

He came up to me and hit me so hard I saw black and white dots. I think I passed out for a second.

Right then and there I decided to run. I couldn't tell any of my friends. They were too meek to understand.

So now here I was, standing on the worst street of a city that hummed with Alpha power and Omega submission, feeling stupid, helpless and weak.

Because I had nothing else to do, and still no plan, I shifted my pack on my shoulder, bent forward slightly, and followed the Alpha who smelled like autumn nights.

# Chapter Two

*Tarin*

Old Town at night was like a zoo where the keepers had all gone away. Not my thing. But that was where Kee hung out, so I found myself scouring the streets for his unruly mop of raven hair and sassy walk.

As I expected, Kee was a no-show. He hadn't answered his texts in close to six months, so I'd gone out for the tenth time in as many weeks to try to find him on the streets. Nothing.

Kee was unreliable at best, and half-mad from drugs, but I had invited him into my household as a ward anyway. Normally, the Omegas I let stay in my guest rooms and whom I sponsored for better lives were there because I wanted to see them thrive and learn. I never slept with a ward. I kept that part of my life separate. But Kee was different.

I met Kee at a club where I was looking for a willing Burn partner. We got a hotel room and he'd serviced me so eagerly and so well, I couldn't get him off my mind. I kept his contact information and used him two more times. Because of our rapport, when I realized he had no permanent house, and hoping maybe we could develop something more, I invited him into my home.

But he remained wild and disobedient to my house rules, and refused to look at the future, let alone study for a trade like the other Omegas I sponsored.

But when I entered my Burns, Kee was always there, lovely and willing, so I used him when he came around. I gave him money and clothes. I bent to his sly will.

My other Omega boys hated him, but they didn't run things. I did. So I let Kee stay when he wanted.

He wasn't quite all there in the head, and I told myself I was doing what I could to help him. I always give him a stack of money. I always told him if he needed anything, to call me. He never did. He was too wild. Too bent on some notion of independence he had neither the sense nor intelligence to fully understand. And he was an addict. I knew it would be his quick downfall. But I kept hoping he'd wake up and see another way.

Now, and for weeks without hearing from him, I couldn't help but worry something had happened to him. Old Town was dangerous at best, and Omegas on their own got into frequent trouble, usually as victims. When I met him, Kee had already succumbed to the lure of the drugs and fast thrills and there was simply no settling him into any other life the way other Omegas I brought home did.

A lot of the Omegas I rescued were so young, and each had his own set of problems. But none quite so difficult—and alluring—as Kee.

Tonight, as I approached a group of hard-looking Omegas hanging out by the corner Kee would often frequent, they all eagerly lifted their faces to me for sex. For money. For a good time.

But that wasn't why I was there.

"Do any of you know an Omega who goes by the name of Kee?"

Disappointed that I wasn't a potential customer, they all shook their heads. But one came forward.

"Kee's not been around for a while, Alpha, but I could show you a good time."

"Do you know where he might have gone?"

The boy shook his head but he looked glum, like he knew. Something bad had happened.

"Thank you." I handed him a hundred dollar bill.

The others on the corner offered themselves again, but I shook my head.

I had my heart set on finding Kee, thinking I might be able to get him to stay this time around. Be stricter with him. Settle him. It was a stupid fantasy on my part. It had already been six months. He wasn't interested in settling down. And I'd never even felt the stirrings of a bond with him because he was so closed off.

For my upcoming Burn this time, less than two weeks away, I'd have to make use of a chattel farm. It wasn't as exciting as having Kee in my bed. The farm Omegas were far too nice for my tastes, too clean-cut and proper and mechanical. Boring.

Well, that would be what would have to happen this time around.

As I made my way down the sidewalk in the growing dusk, past more hustlers beckoning in the windows of sex shops, and through the scent of weed coming from the tattoo parlors, a prickle began high on the back of my neck.

Sidestepping barkers for strip clubs and lingerers at the entrances to bars where loud music thumped and blared into the night, I hurried a little faster toward Uptown where I'd left my Jaguar in a secure and fancy underground garage.

The prickle on my neck grew and tingled at the top of my spine.

Someone trailed me about a hundred yards back. I smelled his silken sweet Omega skin, all natural, not made up and reeking with cologne like the corner boys. I could almost picture him without looking: loose pants, ratty jacket that was probably stolen, a backpack that held all the treasures he owned.

I didn't sense anything malicious. I wasn't scared. I was Alpha; I could take care of myself. I simply didn't want any hassle tonight. And my mood at not being able to find Kee yet again was morose at best.

Another block up and the sounds of the Trenches diminished to echoes and distant hums. All my Alpha senses strained and now I could hear him and smell him much better.

His footfalls came soft and fast, but hesitant. He still smelled sweet but an overlay of musk from unwashed hair and clothes curled around him. It was strangely enticing, and that response was so unlike me.

My car was still half a block up, but I dodged around a closed storefront where a small driveway led to an alley of private parking for the stores that backed up to it.

The footsteps slowed, but came closer all the same.

When I heard him approach the building's edge, I jumped around the corner and put him up against a wall so fast he didn't have time to blink.

My palm connected with his slim throat, holding him taut, and he flailed a little as I pressed my large body to his smaller one. He stopped fighting when he realized he couldn't move.

My face was about two inches from his. Frightened brown eyes stared up at me. His brown hair hung in tangles about his cheeks and head. Maybe he was eighteen. Maybe.

"Why are you following me?" I hissed.

"I—I—" He choked a little.

Realizing I was pressing a bit hard on his airway, I let up. "Answer me. Have you heard something about me? That I'm soft on Omegas? What do you want?"

He sucked in air which puffed up his narrow chest. "I—I thought maybe you were in the market for--" He gulped.

"An Omega? You, maybe?" I almost laughed. I took a half-step back and looked him up and down.

I had no space left in my house right now for any more down and out Omega runaway guests. The spare rooms were all taken. Except Kee's room.

My prediction of this one's appearance had been spot on. He wore a jeans jacket with half the sleeve drooping, a gaping hole at his shoulder. His backpack was slung sideways and squashed between himself and the wall. And his pants were loose, although I had not expected them to be the black drawstring variety the Omegas from chattel farms always wore. He also wore the white chattel shirt, a button up. It looked dingy in the low light, and too thin for the cool night air.

"Another runaway," I accused.

"No, sir. I, uh, I live and work just down there." He nodded back toward the Trenches.

"How long have you been out?"

His dark eyebrows came together to form a tiny dent in the skin between them. "Out?"

"Outside. Away from your babysitter."

"I'm *not* a baby!"

Now I did laugh. "Tell me again why you're following me. Do you know who I am? Did someone send you?"

He sniffed, lifting his chin. "I can show you a good time." His voice came out shaky.

A sudden wind gust filled with dust and smog stirred my hair, pushing my long bangs into my eyes. I stepped back, tossing my head. "Really?"

He blinked slowly. Did he even know how vulnerable he looked right now? My heart skipped with a bit of pity, a bit of empathy.

He was half-trembling, but wouldn't let up. "I saw you at the corner talking to the other boys. They're not like me, though. I'm different."

I looked back at his black trousers. "Farm trained, I'm sure. Did you even stick around to have your first time?"

"I am farm trained. So what? And no I didn't stick around. That's why I tell you I can be good for you. First time and all. It will cost a little more, but I'll be good. I swear."

I could hear his stomach growling from where I stood. He was hungry. Tired. A curl of fear swept through his gaze before vanishing as he again blinked those big dark eyes at me.

Tonight was not a good night for me. I was not in rescue mode. The Omegas I already had at the house were a handful. As for sex, I had come to find Kee and no one else. Without Kee, I made use of the farms.

Now this little Omega stood in front of me with his puppy eyes and his growling stomach—

No. It was not going to happen. I didn't like virgins. Not for my Burns and not for any time in between. At the farms I always paid for the older ones. And Kee had been well broken in long before I met him.

"Four walls. A roof. The farms aren't prisons. Why run?" I asked him. Surely starving and selling himself in a world that led to hard risks and no hope for glamour from those Trench shadows was worse than anything he came from.

But every Omega had their sad story. Here was another about to begin. I wanted to turn away. I *needed* to turn away. I didn't have time for this. But something kept my boots rooted to the spot.

"I hated it there, that's all." He shuffled his feet.

Well, he was going to hate it more on the streets. But I didn't tell him that.

"Are you even eighteen?"

He brightened a little at my question. "I turn eighteen tomorrow."

"Great." I faked my smile. He was surely not having a happy birthday from what I could see.

Again, something tugged in my chest. Maybe it was his sweet look. Maybe it was his fresh, cookie dough scent.

I was the complete opposite of those Omega-hating Alphas who think all Omegas are trash, or good for only one thing. For one thing, I had a heart. But if I tried to rescue every Omega I saw, I'd need a farm myself. I was rich, but not that rich.

I could only handle three or four Omegas at a time. Right now I had three, not counting Kee. Two were lovers and took up only one spare room. They studied hard and were learning accounting. I'd eventually find them both a job and

14

sponsor them, remaining their financial guardian since they weren't allowed to have bank accounts of their own.

My other Omega guest had his own room, and was studying to be a legal secretary. He was smart enough, he might actually make it to licensed paralegal.

And then Kee had a room, but he was in and out so often—mostly out—and studied nothing. I had to come to terms with the fact that he was not really living with me.

"So, well, uh," the boy stuttered. It was annoyingly cute. He put his hands on his hips, elbows out, and cocked his hip. "I'm Alli. Should we talk price, or not?"

"Oh, well now. Look at you. Now I'm inclined to think you're lying about being a virgin."

His eyes widened in shock. "I am one!"

Of course I could see he wasn't lying. He wasn't street smart enough for that yet. But I said, "Uh huh. Growing up with all those cute Omega boys. I'm sure you've fooled around." I knew I was being hard on him, but I was stupidly missing Kee. And I didn't need to be bamboozled by another hard luck case.

The muscles hardened beneath his eyes. "I just—what do I need to do? I mean, either you believe me or not."

"Some advice if you're going to sell yourself down here. Make sure of your market first."

"What? You came to the Trenches. You were talking with those other boys. I saw."

"I was looking for someone." I looked him up and down, tightening my gaze. "Not you."

He shuffled from one foot to the other. "So why are you talking to me—"

I shushed him with one hand raised fast to his face. "Let's get something straight here. You followed me. You thought I looked like a good prospect to—what?—rob? You're too little and too young to take on an Alpha like me, so you'd do it coyly, through seduction. You'd get to my house and do whatever was necessary to get what you need. Steal it. Maybe even put out for it."

"I'm not a thief!" he countered. "Fine. I get it now. You're not in the market."

I let out a chuckle as his face screwed up all cute and even more child-like. I didn't like them young, but damn, all those tangles of brown hair, and those fawn-colored eyes, and resting behind that was look a spirit of a boy who'd had enough of everything but was still desperate, still hungry. That drive could change a person, make them trip an old man for an apple.

"You need to learn a few things if you're going to survive on the streets," I said.

"Fuck you," he replied, and turned away, shifting his backpack, tossing his head.

The way he held his chin up and shoved one hand through the mass on his head. The way he put his shoulders back, even as he huffed so hard I could hear his breath though his back was to me. And that scent of him, like something warm from the oven, sweet and fresh—it tugged.

I wasn't immune to cute. I wasn't immune to Omegas down on their luck or I wouldn't have them as guests in my home and sponsor them. I had no discriminations, not against the ones in the Trenches or the runaways most thought were garbage and would amount to no more than addicts and criminals.

If only I were better at resisting their suffering.

I sighed hard. Then heard myself blurt, "Alli! Are you hungry?"

He stopped hard in his tracks, his back still to me. Silence.

"Come on," I said. "I can at least get you something to eat."

He turned slowly. "What for?"

I shrugged. "Because I'm here and you need food and I can give you that. Should there be any other reason?"

16

"Nothing is free."

"No. Nothing is free. You are going to have to look at me while you eat your burger. You're going to listen to me, too, when I tell you some things."

"What things?"

"Whatever I want."

"And then what?" Those cute eyes squinted in suspicion.

"And maybe by then I'll decide what to do with you."

A renewed eagerness lit his eyes. "I really am trained. Farm trained. And I really am a virgin," he said walking toward me.

I cuffed his jacket sleeve. "Shut up and let's go."

"Is your Burn coming up? Is that why you were looking for someone?"

"Did I say shut up? I think I did." I grabbed his sleeve tighter and pushed him a little in front of me.

His scent alarmed me with its potency. Street boys usually didn't affect me too much, aside from my do-gooder heart and the empathy that made me open my house to a few of them. But right now, something in the air had changed. It was this Omega, and my gut told me not to do this. I should just give him a hundred and tell him to go.

But I kept pushing him up the street toward the parking lot and my car.

Hunger gnawed at my insides, and not for food. I don't remember an Omega affecting me this strongly and this quickly before, especially one who had slept in alley refuse and hadn't bathed in who knew how long.

I kept telling myself he wasn't my type. Too young. Too desperate. Too inexperienced. His needs focused on survival and not me. My bleeding heart could buy him a burger, I had no inner quarrel with that. But deeper urges I wanted to ignore wrestled and shoved their way through my body. So unlike me.

Shit.

# Chapter Three

*Alli*

Maybe I should have been scared. Maybe going off with a stranger Alpha was the worst possible decision of my life, aside from trying to take on a revered and tenured housedad no matter how twisted and nasty he was.

I'd been stupid and made a lot of mistakes.

I told myself I had no more choices. I'd already made the decision I would never allow myself to be institutionalized. But now I was starving and with no prospects but selling myself. Or other criminal activity if I could rob this Alpha. But he'd already told me he was on guard about that. Going off with this guy whose name I still didn't know was certainly not the worst case scenario I could be facing.

Unless he was a serial killer. But even then, what did I have to lose? My life? It was nothing right now if I didn't get some food and a good night's sleep.

The car was jet black, looked new, and some make and model I knew little about but could see right away was expensive. When the Alpha opened the passenger door and ushered me in, the new leather and fresh scent of window wash hit me hard. I breathed in. After the smell on the streets, acrid and dusty and rotting, my lungs heaved in gulps of oxygen untainted by Old Town fumes and toxins.

The Alpha pulled his car out of the garage with a little squeal, though he wasn't going fast. The floor was shiny and smooth, and the car was probably brand new. The entry was gated, but the arm lifted for him as if it recognized him, no problem.

For five minutes we drove. He took a freeway that I thought looked like it might lead back to Zilly's Omega Farm. A needle-like pain stabbed my chest as I pictured all this as a trap and him taking me back there and leaving me.

"Where are we going?"

He pulled off the freeway and I saw the bright sign of a diner. "Here."

My breath came a little fast in relief. Not a trap.

I heard the locks click as the engine turned off, and tried my door. It opened easily.

As the Alpha came around the front of the car, I noted again how big he was, how his pale blue eyes glinted under the parking lights beneath a fall of dark hair that curved over his left eyebrow and mixed perfectly with the rest of his glossy hair. His body was lean-waisted, but I could see muscles pulling at his sleeves and at the thighs of his jeans.

Something stirred inside me. The way he smelled—everything—it was almost annoying. Because maybe I wanted him, but didn't want to want him beyond what I could get right now. A meal. A bed. Maybe some cash.

He led the way to the diner's entrance and I had to hurry to catch up.

"Hey, you never told me your name."

"No," he replied.

I let out a flustered groan.

He turned. "You going to behave?"

My stomach growled. I growled, "Whatever you want."

The restaurant had farm décor all over the walls and counters, and I was so not impressed for my first time entering a diner. Little trellises covered with fake vines, tiny shovels with ribbons on the ends, wooden cutouts of pastel painted chickens and pigs. The booths were baby pink and blue. It was the last place I thought this Alpha would want to be.

But when we were seated, he said, "The burgers here are the best I've ever had."

"Oh. Okay."

"And my name is Tarin."

"Oh, um." I hated that I could think of no words to respond. *Tarin.* I liked how the name rippled in my mind.

The waiter handed us square plastic sheets the size of a large book that folded open with lists of food items, some accompanied by pictures. I studied my sheet wondering what it meant. I'd never been in a place like this before. I wasn't sure what to expect. Starting at the top, I began to read every word so this Alpha wouldn't think I was stupid as well as pathetic.

As the waiter brought water, Tarin said, "We're ready to order." He looked at me over his menu.

"Uh, uh--" I'd barely gotten through reading the third item offered, which was still under a heading called *Appetizers.*

"You are helpless, aren't you?" Tarin said, picking up my menu.

"I've never been outside like this."

"I see that." He handed my menu to the waiter and for a moment I thought I'd missed my chance and wouldn't get any food.

Instead, he ordered for me. "He'll have a bacon cheeseburger, chili fries, and large lemon-lime soda."

My eyes widened.

"What?" he asked. "You don't like that?"

My stomach growled. I shook my head. "No. It's fine." The funny thing was, it's what I would have ordered for myself if I'd known how to do it.

I drank down my ice water as we waited for the food and drinks.

Tarin watched me, one sleek, dark eyebrow cocked. His eyes really were remarkable, the color of fresh pool water in sunlight, a wonderfully lighter contrast to his dark brown hair.

"Tell me what you're doing out there in the Trenches when you're obviously smarter than that."

For a moment, I thought: *None of your business.*

But when he called me smart, I stopped the thought. Something about him—force, brawn, intensity all combined even when I first glimpsed him on the dusty corners talking to the rent boys—was already crashing through my defenses like he deserved to have whatever he asked for. Including my thoughts.

Before I knew it, words poured from my mouth. I tried to keep my tone clipped, flat, but my breaths were coming faster and faster as I told him about my teen years, being pestered and tormented by a house-dad who hated me, who tied up my cock, and then finding out he was raping some boys and how if I told, I'd be institutionalized. Same if I fought back. The house-dad had all the power, but with no responsibility for it or us.

"I hated him. He was going to send me to an institution. Or I'd have a life of janitor duty at the farm and never meet an Alpha ever! I couldn't stay!" I realized my voice came out hard and defensive. "I'd rather starve on the streets than go to a loony bin."

"That sounds tough," he said quietly.

"Doesn't every kid on the street have a sob story?" I asked.

"Sure. A lot of people not on the streets as well," he replied.

I nervously chewed my lower lip but did not look away. "Yeah, well."

"I say that not to diminish your experience. Just pointing it out."

I nodded tightly, and was proud I didn't feel any tears. Not that I wasn't above crying to get sympathy. But the real tears—I didn't want him to see the real tears.

When the food came, I couldn't believe how good it smelled. The burger fresh and hot and still sizzling, the fries smothered in beanless chili with melted cheese on top.

I dived in and my saliva glands instantly flooded my mouth, dissolving the food so fast I practically drank it.

"Slow down," Tarin said. His voice broke through my calorie high, soft but firm.

I gulped down the bite in my mouth and picked up my drink. The sweetness flowed through me. Lemon-lime. How did he know it was my favorite?

All I remembered about the rest of the meal was an overwhelming need to fill my belly, along with a heavy, dark presence before me who I now thought of as my rescuer, my savior. A neediness for more than food came over me and I was scared that after the meal, this would all end. He would go away and leave me behind.

I wanted to latch myself to him somehow, follow him home like a wayward stray. I actually had the thought I'd sit on the steps of his house if I had to, night and day through rain and heat, and wait for him to see my worth.

Damn it, I was stronger than that.

Tarin ate his own burger at a leisurely pace. I sat very still, my food all gone, and it felt like I was waiting for my life to end. I wanted to linger, prolong the inevitable, for I knew after we were done, Tarin would drive away. Maybe he'd give me some money; I wasn't sure. But of course he had better things to do than worry about me. I was an adult now—well, as of tomorrow officially—and I needed to deal as an adult and learn to take care of myself.

But Omegas had everything going against them in this world. We couldn't hold down anything but menial jobs that offered few if any benefits unless we paid to learn a trade, and none of us had money. Even then, we couldn't have bank accounts unless we had guardians and those services didn't come cheap. Everything was stacked against us if we were single and unbonded.

The waiter brought me another lemon-lime soda, and I sipped it slowly, flicking my eyes up and down, watching Tarin without trying to look like I was staring at him, assessing his mannerisms, the way he chewed his food, how he swallowed slowly so his Adam's apple bobbed enticingly.

He was big and I couldn't help but wonder what it might feel like to have his tall, muscular body wrapped around me, encasing me, tightening so I couldn't be free even if I wanted to.

I'd be dead if I said it didn't intrigue me. He was handsome and did not hesitate to tell me what to do, what to order off the menu, or how wrong I might be in assuming he even wanted an Omega boy right now.

But he'd plucked me up as if, despite my Omega status, I was worthy at least of having a decent meal. He'd led and I'd followed like I'd been trained to do. The thought of that made me a little angry and a little relieved at the same time. I'd be lying if I said I wasn't lost. But I also wanted him to see I wasn't some pushover Omega farm boy.

As he swallowed the last French fry from his plate, and sipped the iced dregs of his cola, I felt my eyes grow warm. It was all ending too quickly. The little meal in the stupid restaurant with a country barn motif was going to be but a memory and I would no doubt soon be back in my alley sitting up all night huddled against my backpack trying to stay warm.

I inhaled sharply.

Tarin glanced sharply at me, but his eyes softened. "Did you want dessert?"

It was too much. I was already over-full, but I didn't want to leave yet. I nodded.

Again, he ordered for me. Just what I would have ordered myself, if I'd known it was on the menu.

"Two hot fudge sundaes," he said.

He winked at me when the waiter left. "You like hot fudge, don't you?"

I nodded.

By the time the sundae came, I realized I could not stuff another bite into my stomach. But I lifted my spoon and took a taste. I didn't want to show any weakness. Or have any food go to waste. So I forced it down.

It was wonderful. I'd eaten half the sundae before I realized it, and my stomach began to ache. I knew what that meant, and before I could give any warning, I got up and ran to the sign that said *Restrooms*.

I barely got inside before I was throwing up in a stall. Luckily, I didn't make too much of a mess. But damn, it was awful. I gagged until tears streaked my cheeks.

I wiped my face and when I came out of the stall, Tarin was standing by the sink holding my backpack.

"Too much too fast," he said. It was not a question.

I nodded slowly. When I reached for my backpack, my hand was shaking.

He gave it over without a word, then turned and walked out. I followed. What else could I do?

At the car, I hesitated, miserable, my eyes still fogged with tears.

Tarin looked at me. Finally, he spoke. "Get in."

"What?"

"Get in." He opened the passenger door.

"I can walk back."

"To the Trenches?" He shook his head. "No. You're coming home with me. I've got a spare room for the night. You need real sleep. At the very least, you need soda crackers and ginger ale."

Was he for real? He was going to take care of me? He didn't even know me. Would he want more? Payment? I figured I could do it. I was planning on it anyway when I'd first decided to follow him. I could take it. I would demand payment from him for my virginity, too. I could do that. I had a big mouth and a bold spirit. Yeah, I could do it.

24

I took a deep breath, puffing out my chest, blinking away the haze of my nausea. "One night," I agreed. My unspoken thought: *And I'll pay you back. Somehow.*

# Chapter Four

*Tarin*

To see his misbehavior—eating too much too fast. To see his tears. Why did that make my insides twist and my heart pound?

He didn't remind me of Kee in any way. He was determined, but not so wild. He wanted to have his own way, but he wasn't an addict.

I wanted to cuff him like an errant child. I wanted to pull him to me and hold him until he stopped shaking.

He had a desperation about him, and that had made him eat everything I'd ordered for him too fast and get sick.

A lot of Alphas would think: *He's an Omega; he doesn't know better.*

Not me. I knew Omegas had a lot going against them, but they weren't stupid. They could think and reason and they didn't have to act foolish and needy all the time. It was a trained role, an expectation put onto them by their upbringing, and by this world which in so many ways told them they were less than efficient, not whole without an Alpha around to complete them.

I wanted to coddle him at the same time I wanted to reprimand. The oddness of it made my stomach flutter in a way Kee never had. I cared about Kee, but Kee was his own boy and would never be mine even if I'd wanted that. Kee wasn't the Omega for me, and never had been.

But damn it, this one affected me when my initial plan had been to *not* get involved.

In the car, Alli sat very still, head down, clutching his backpack.

Every part of me wanted to reach out to him. It wasn't like me to feel this way, more than empathy, more than a bleeding heart do-gooder attitude.

With Kee, it had been about sex from the beginning. I'd wanted to give him more, but I didn't have what he needed. He wanted to escape. He wanted a high. He wanted freedom without even knowing what the word meant.

I'd been able to give that to Kee if nothing more. He'd never been emotionally or sexually responsive to me outside my Burn, nor I to him beyond the habit of looking for him days before my next scheduled Burn. He liked me because I filled his pockets with bills and gave him his brand of freedom for a few more days or weeks, a few more highs.

But Alli had a different pull, a unique scent. He was a miserable little runaway with no sense having escaped from a structured environment that had threatened him.

Institutionalization was cruel. I had no doubts that his house-dad who abused him and his brothers would have made good on his threat. But Alli had run away to a not much better life in the Trenches. He was young and without a plan. Different from Kee.

Why was I comparing the two of them?

I had a Burn coming up. Of course I needed an Omega for that. And Alli had been on offer. But that had been because of his hunger. His exhaustion. It was against all my principles to take advantage of that.

I had a firm hold on myself. I didn't take Omegas into my home to fuck them. It had only ever happened with Kee, and only because Kee was a previous Burn partner.

But now something else was happening. It annoyed me to find I wasn't so pure as to not think of Alli in that light. His potent scent had struck me—sweet and tempting—but he'd been all mouth and desperation when he'd made his offer to me of his virginity. I didn't want to take advantage of that. Honestly. Virgins weren't my thing.

But his soft brown hair and the way he'd scrunched up his face as he read the restaurant menu, something he'd never seen before since it was his first time in a diner, made my chest tighten.

I wasn't a bad man. Not with all the good I had done in the world. But sometimes I had bad thoughts.

Fifteen minutes later I pulled into my driveway.

Alli looked up as the garage door sensor automatically opened to my Jag, his eyes big and bright.

"You live here? In this big house all by yourself?"

I nodded. "I do. But not all by myself."

He frowned. "You have kids? Or a bond mate?"

I shook my head. "They aren't my kids. But I have some guests."

"Oh. How old are you?"

I looked at him, one eyebrow raised. "Why?"

"Why don't you have a bond mate? You're set for life. You've got it all." He gestured toward the house and the spacious garage where my second car, a red Ferrari, sat.

"That's a lot of questions," I replied.

"Well, you're taking me inside and I don't know you. Maybe something is wrong with you. Like up here." Alli tapped the side of his head. "Maybe you're going to kill me and bury me in your backyard."

"When you live on the streets, that's a risk, isn't it?" I said quietly.

He frowned. "Are you a murderer?"

"No. But if I were, do you think I'd admit it?"

He made an annoyed grunt and glanced warily around as the garage lights came on and I drove in. The door came down behind us.

I opened my door and turned toward him. "I have no intention of seeing you hurt. As I said, I have a guest room. You were sick and you need rest."

"What if *I'm* a murderer?" he asked smartly.

"Well, then I'd defend myself." I looked him up and down. "What are you, a hundred and thirty pounds soaking wet?"

"Who are your guests?"

"You will meet them in good time."

He said nothing to that, and opened his door, getting out and standing under the garish light of my garage. It was sparkling clean, just as I liked it, everything in its place.

As we walked into the house through the door that led to the kitchen, Alli's mouth opened as he took in my massive black and silver counters and cupboards, and the vast dining room and living room beyond.

Even as he looked around, though, I saw his feet dragging. His pack hung loose on his left arm. He was exhausted.

"How about I give you a tour in the morning?"

He looked at me, eyebrows down. "I thought you might be rich. But—wow."

"What? Did my car give it away?"

He shook his head. "It wasn't even your clothes, but the way you walked. Even the way you held yourself around the Omega Trench boys."

"I'm an Alpha," I said as if that explained it.

He shrugged. "And when you first spoke. Like the words felt more proper or something."

"How many Alphas have you met?"

"Not many." He ducked his head. "Not any, actually."

"Really? I never would have guessed," I said.

He shut his mouth into a tight line.

"Come on. Let me show you your room. You'll have Kee's room until he returns."

"Who's Kee?"

"Just someone I was looking for tonight. But I don't think he'll be back. You'll like the room. It's the nicest one upstairs. The other boys live in the two bedrooms downstairs."

Alli followed me up the stairs, his steps slow and controlled. Three days on the streets might not sound like a lot, but to an innocent, farm-raised boy it could feel like a year. He had been starving and now found himself in a strange place. Oddly, I wanted to sweep him into my arms and carry him, but that would have been completely ridiculous.

I opened the first door in the hall to my upstairs guest room and turned on the light. "It still has some things in it from the other boy in the closet. Please don't touch them. I'll get you your own clothes. Otherwise, it's been recently cleaned top to bottom." I had a housekeeper in twice a week.

Alli's mouth opened wide again to see the sumptuous pillows on the bed, the décor all sea greens and blues, Kee's favorite colors.

"You have your own private bath," I said. "Check the drawer under the sink if you need a toothbrush and comb and other stuff. They're new. Do you shave? Most Omegas don't, but some do."

He shook his head.

"Towels are hanging. They're clean. There are shampoos and soaps on a tray in the shower."

"Wow."

"In the bathroom closet you'll find a spare, clean robe."

It wasn't Kee's. He never wore robes. And around me, in our closed rooms, he often went naked.

"Do you need anything else?" I asked.

As if in a daze, Alli shook his head.

"I'll bring you up some ginger ale. All right?"

He nodded as I turned to leave, keeping the door slightly ajar as I went.

When I returned with a tray containing the drink and some saltine crackers, he was just coming out of the bathroom, his face still shiny from a cursory wash. He'd taken off his shoes and jacket. The white shirt was unbuttoned down the front.

He looked tousled and exhausted.

I set the tray on the nightstand. "This will settle your stomach."

He came to the edge of the bed, looking down. "You don't have to take care of me."

"Someone does."

He looked up. "I—I—thank you."

"My room is next door. If you need me, don't hesitate to come in and wake me."

"I would never do that," he said flatly.

"You will if you need anything. Do you understand?" I tried to sound firm.

"I mean, all this." He spread his arms, then looked longingly at the bed. "What do you do for a living?"

"Questions. So many questions. We'll talk in the morning, all right?"

He nodded, weary, looking on the verge of collapse. What more could I do for him?

I had the most annoying thought I wanted him with me, in my bed, sleeping where I could keep an eye on him, put my arms around him, prevent him from getting into any trouble.

Again, this wasn't like me. I didn't take advantage of my Omegas.

But I felt the strangest sensation with Alli. The sexual energy was there, but I kept trying to convince myself to dismiss it as mere Alpha to Omega reaction, nothing more.

I had protective instincts for Omegas in general. It was in my Alpha DNA, along with the hormones. But wanting to protect any down and out individual wasn't unique or rare. At least, not if you weren't a sociopath or an Omega-hater.

But with Alli it was more. This was me wanting to— what?—mark him, make him smell like he was mine so no one else would ever touch him.

With Kee I never thought about marking him specifically, because I knew he went with other Alphas. The other Omegas I had sponsored had come with numbers of problems that did not attract me in any way more than an instinct to help. I had chosen them to come live with me for their qualities that included intelligence, strength of will, and a seeming willingness to want another life. Most lost and homeless Omegas were embittered and enraged beyond rationality. I used my instinct to choose who I wanted to mentor.

With Alli, he had chosen me. He had followed me. I had wanted to reject him outright. I had wanted to go on with my evening without extra drama, hoping Kee might finally text me.

Then Alli appeared. I kept telling myself the kid was not my type. Not tempting. And yet he was when I finally got a whiff of him. When I turned my full, unwavering attention on him and realized I wasn't the type to feed him, make him sick on the rich foods, then dump him, I also felt the other pull. It wasn't like it was with Kee, either, but something else, something more.

Now, as I half-closed the door to his bedroom, I had the urge again to want him near. I wanted to build walls around him—not literally, but mentally. I wanted to know he was close and thriving and not alone.

I turned away, brushing it all off as me feeling sorry for him. His story sucked, like most Omegas' stories. His hunger and runaway status and needy, friendless state merely filled me with empathy. Plus, I was days away from my Burn. It made me overly sensitive.

Those were the excuses I made to myself.

I went into my bedroom and prepared for bed. It was early for me yet. But something was stirring in me. Something restless, like a storm on the horizon.

The Burn. Yes, that's what it was. It had to be that and only that dragging me earlier than normal into a pre-fever state where I needed quiet, calm, low light, maybe a good book before expending a lot of my energy over the two to three days that ruled my sexual fevers.

In the shower I discovered myself hard, convincing myself it was because I'd been expecting Kee tonight for some pre-Burn activity—and I quickly took care of it.

Sensitive. I was so sensitive.

As I touched myself, I reeled. More than usual. I could feel the presence in the room just next door, young and unsure, exhausted and alone. I saw his silken tangles of brunet mop, the hairless angles of his thin chest where his shirt was unbuttoned as he'd come out of the bathroom.

I imagined he'd be cool to the touch for his first time, then hot. Real hot. His skin thin over his bones, the ridges of his ribs moving up and down as his breath quickened, his belly concave and small enough that my palm would fit over it perfectly, pressing a little as if to hold him down.

He'd be hard and his cock would be medium sized, not too big, like I liked my Omegas, not too heavy, and it would stand up straight all on its own without needing the support of an encircled thumb and forefinger around the base. The foreskin would still be there, as was the current common trend for Omegas—whereas Alphas were cut half the time for no reason I could see.

That foreskin would be young and unstretched, and pulled back taut without much work exposing his head, the dampness there, the body's longing.

He would spread his legs and there would be a hint of a shine behind his balls. He'd lift himself and his legs even more to expose that wanton Omega hole…

I didn't even know I was consciously thinking all these things until I came fast and hard, without much effort, the shower washing the copious amounts of semen that kept jetting from me down the drain.

Depleted, my body felt better. But my mind still sensed him. Like he was merely a breath away.

No Omega had had that much effect on me outside the Burn, or so quickly.

It had to be his sorry state. It couldn't be his youth since I preferred them a little broken in. It wasn't his virginity. I was less than patient during my Burns. So what was it?

I got into my bed naked, and picked up my tablet, looking to distract myself from further worry and thoughts about it.

An hour later, though it was still early, my eyelids drooped. I waved out the lights and pulled up the covers, turning on my side.

Sleep came quickly.

# Chapter Five

## *Alli*

When I was little, my Omega caretaker in the Children's Wing of Zilly's Chattel Farm would give me ginger ale when I felt sick. I loved it. He'd sit with me and rub my head or shoulders as I sat in bed and drank. I was safe and needed for nothing.

Now that sensation returned as I lay back against the sumptuous pillows of Tarin's guest room and drank the ginger ale in slow sips. For a time, my sense of displacement went away. My hunger abated—though I had thrown up nearly all I'd eaten—and my stomach quieted.

The soda crackers suddenly looked like heaven. I ate two.

My mind stopped spinning. I relished in the clean sheets, the warmth away from the cold nights I'd spent outside, and the peacefulness of an elaborate home that seemed like a dream. The rich Alpha who'd owned it seemed like a dream, as well.

It had only been three nights in all that I'd been out, but it had felt like three months. I'd been so miserable.

That was why I'd followed the Alpha in the first place. Desperation. At least that's what I told myself.

But that autumn scent of him mixed me up. I'd followed on instinct, not just desperation. My logic veered off from simple need and my feet were moving in his direction as if of their own volition as he moved away from the more dangerous corners of the Trenches.

Like a magnet, my body was pulled by his. Longings from deep inside started to spark into something new. Something I'd only glimpsed, or felt on a very magical night, or from some beautiful dream I'd awakened from that faded fast as I opened my eyes.

That sort of thing—it couldn't be real. I didn't want it to be real because if it was something not from my hunger-fed imagination, then I was vulnerable. I could be hurt even more than I ever thought possible. Because that sensation, it felt like everything I was and ever could be. It made me feel as if I had something to lose, and that was a horrifying thought.

Tarin was a wall away. It felt close but far at the same time, and I wanted to sense him with more than my mind. I wanted touch, scent, sound—to hear him breathe, to see him blink his sky-hued eyes with his sole focus on me.

I hadn't actually met an Alpha before. Not one on one. I wondered if it was normal for an Omega to feel this way around them.

Tarin had literally rescued me. Of course I'd feel affection toward him for that. I'd probably even feel some sort of awe. That alone explained a lot.

My thoughts kept me restless for a while, but exhaustion finally took over.

Morning light bled through the curtains when I next opened my eyes. I had slept so soundly, I hadn't moved from the spot I was in when I fell to sleep. I had no sense of time.

Blinking, I saw a digital clock on the nightstand. *7:53.*

I got up and rummaged through my backpack for a clean shirt and trousers. The only ones I had were the usual farm uniform: black pants, white button up. After showering, I put on my cleaner clothes.

Barefoot, I went to the door and peeked into the hallway. I heard no sound, but I smelled coffee and bacon from downstairs.

Following my nose, I found the kitchen we'd walked through last night. Three boys a little older than I sat around a large wooden table decorated with flowers and candlesticks. Tarin stood at a stove making breakfast. For some reason I'd expected him, rich as he was, to order out, or have a chef.

36

"Are you hungry?" he asked me casually, as if I'd lived there for days.

"Yes."

"Sit." He indicated the occupied table. "Boys, introduce yourselves, please. This is Alli."

Two were reading tablets. One was handwriting scribbles in a notebook. They all looked up.

"I'm Oren," said the first, a serious-looking young man with black glasses and close cropped pale hair.

"I'm Farrell and this is Tev," said the next. The two sat very close together, like a couple, and even looked similar with their dark blond hair and square, handsome faces.

"Hi." I felt suddenly all too shy, and my face heated. They were more mature than my Omega brothers back on the farm, more focused, less hyper.

They all nodded, watching me for a moment as I sat.

I expected a barrage of questions, or at the very least some suspicious looks, but they seemed immediately accepting, as if new guys came in to the house to live every day.

I wondered how long they'd been here, but I was too shy to ask anything right now. All Tarin had told me was they were his guests.

Where I sat, I faced a lovely window overlooking a bed of flowers and a white trellis supporting strands of ivy. I tried to focus on that and nothing else, but my mind spiraled with curiosity. Had these guys slept with Tarin? Were they a sort of on-call team for his Burns?

My stomach growled.

When Tarin put a plate of eggs, bacon and toast in front of me, I tried not to inhale it. I was so hungry. I downed half a glass of orange juice in a single gulp.

"Remember last night and slow down," Tarin said, sitting with his own plate of eggs, bacon and toast after serving the other guys.

Everyone dug into their food without comment.

I made myself chew slowly as I tried not to devour everything at once. A bite of toast, then egg, then bacon. My mouth ached from all the lovely flavors.

Everything here was quiet, safe, peaceful. I could grow to love it but I couldn't allow myself to become used to it. It was too much. It was everything. And no doubt I'd be leaving soon, losing it all, because Tarin hadn't formally invited me to be his guest yet. None of this was mine.

But for now, I could at least enjoy a real breakfast after one day of protein bars and two days of nothing but my rationed water.

Again, I had so many questions bubbling up in my mind, but I stayed quiet. I almost didn't want to know the answers. I didn't want anything to change this peace right now. This comfort-feeling.

Tarin interrupted my silence. "Alli, you had many questions last night."

I looked up at him, swallowing hard. The others glanced up as well, looking on as if to see what might happen and witness my fate at failing to measure up and being turned loose all too soon.

"Are you still interested in this place, in being here?"

I took a breath, straightened. "Are you? In me, I mean?" I wasn't brave enough to ask, *Do I meet your standards?*

Both his sleek black eyebrows rose slightly. "Yes, I have questions for you, too."

My body trembled at the idea. Questions scared me. I was afraid he'd lose his patience with me and dismiss me too quickly the way Gray had, Gray who had never liked anything I had to say, Gray who called me argumentative and accused me of things I'd never done.

I waited for Tarin to continue, thinking he might begin interrogating me in front of the others, but he showed no sign of further interest, focusing again on his food.

I had stopped eating and stared at him. After he had a few forkfuls of eggs, he looked up at me.

"Did you have any prospects in mind when you ran away?"

*Get away from my pervert of a house-dad.* I thought quickly about giving the right answer. Aloud, I said, "Find an Alpha benefactor, I guess."

"Most who hunt the Trenches aren't looking for anything like that."

"I can work. I'm a fast learner and strong. If I could get a job." Were these the right answers? I hoped.

His eyes closed half-way as if he were assessing me deeper. Finally, he gave a heavy sigh.

The other young men were watching him carefully but reverently. Obviously, they'd all been through this.

"You asked last night what I do for a living. I am an engineer. Mostly mechanical and electrical. And I have many patents that pay me royalties."

"That's--" I gulped. "What exactly is an engineer?"

One of the Omegas snickered—Oren—and Tarin shot him a stern look.

"I fix problems," said Tarin. "I make prospects of some scientific applications more marketable."

"You mean you invent stuff?"

He smiled. "Sometimes."

"You seem very smart for your age." My voice came out soft. How old was he anyway? He'd never answered that question last night.

He blinked at me.

"I mean, you have all this." I waved my hand through the air, trying not to look at the other boys, trying not to stutter my thoughts. "And you're young-looking, I mean, I don't know how old you are, but you look young still." Alphas could live to as old as two hundred, while Omega life spans tended to be shorter at one hundred fifty to one hundred seventy-five years.

I continued. "I mean, it's a lot for your age."

I nearly choked on that last statement, not realizing how it sounded until it came out.

"Sorry, I didn't mean that how it sounded."

"It's all right. If you must know, I'm fifty-two."

I balked. It seemed old to me, not age-wise, but in experience. "And you're unbonded?"

That came out way too fast.

Oren got up and took his plate to the sink. I heard the water come on. I heard him put it in the dishwasher.

Tarin focused on his plate, forking scrambled eggs into his mouth as if he hadn't heard me.

Oren said, "I've got a lot of homework today." Without waiting for an answer, he left.

The other two smirked at each other, as if they had some silent telepathic language of their own.

I swallowed a bit of toast and it went down like ash. I'd felt bold one on one on the street with Tarin, but now everything had become awkward, and the energy of the other Omegas was almost off-putting.

No one spoke.

Finally the other two got up and rinsed their plates. They left quietly without comment.

I kept putting food into my mouth and not tasting it even though I was famished.

Everything felt wrong, causing little sparks of panic in my veins. Was Tarin going to kick me out now? I didn't know what to say.

Tarin put a napkin to his lips, then spoke. "You have a lot of questions. I know."

"I am sometimes a bit forward. My house-dad hated me for it." *The perv.*

"Here, in this house, I encourage strength of character and curiosity. But I also teach my boys manners. I'm not a farm. I'm not going to keep you against your will. I'm not here to impose impossible rules and regulations, or hold you back in any way."

40

His words surprised me. I wasn't sure I believed him. He seemed quite dominant. His Omega guests were controlled in their behavior, almost formal.

"As to your question about bond mates, that is quite personal."

My face heated.

"But I will answer. I've had relationships before with Omegas. They never worked out, that's all. You know the factors and issues. Compatibility, bonding ranks, plus most Omegas I meet—not from the Trenches— do not want kids right away and I do."

"Uh, oh. Sorry if it is a sore subject. I just wondered."

"It's not—" He stopped.

"The others left kind of quickly," I said. "I stuck my foot in my mouth, it's obvious."

"They know I went looking for someone last night."

"The one whose room I'm in?"

Tarin nodded. "But he hasn't been back here in weeks. Six months, actually. It's all right. I didn't really expect to find him last night."

I nodded. Then I opened my big damn mouth again. "But you want kids, right?" I asked, feeling my face heat again. Even with Gray's abnormal punishments, I'd never learned when to stop.

"Yes," he said, the corner of his mouth twitching.

"I'm sorry it hasn't worked out for you."

An awkward silence descended over us.

I had always talked too much back at the farm. It was one of the major things that got me into trouble, that and kissing Omega boys—nothing more. I wanted things I couldn't put into words.

When I became a teen, I looked forward to servicing Alphas in their Burn but I also wanted more. Something I couldn't put into words. More than what the other boys talked about all the time: wedding, kids, an Alpha mate.

Sure, I wanted love and all of that. I wanted to know what a bond felt like. But I didn't want it all to look so boring on the outside and be that way on the inside as well. I wanted the excitement of love, but what the hell did that mean? Emotionally? Physically? Sexually? I didn't even know.

"I don't know anything about what I really want. Of course I expected to find my sexual awakening in the mating hall. I looked forward to it. But Gray was going to block that path. I didn't want to go to an institution. That much I knew. I didn't have time to plan anything. Since the warden didn't believe Gray was abusing us, I saw only one option."

"Run." Tarin quickly supplied the answer.

I nodded.

"Did you follow me last night thinking I might pick you up and you could later rob me? Tell the truth. I'll know if you're lying."

How would he know? But I didn't want to lie to him. "I wanted what I could get—what I needed. What's the difference, anyway, between servicing Alphas at the farm and selling it on the street?"

"It's safer at the farms for one thing."

"That's not entirely true," I argued. "I knew one guy who got beat up pretty bad. Almost died before the handlers got into the mating room and put the Alpha out. Then the Alpha came back and tried to make a claim on him."

"I thought we were all screened at the farms."

"You are. But you have all the power. That means all the power to lie and not get caught."

Tarin nodded. "You're right. Well, I'm a fixer, right?"

I gave him a weak smile. "An engineer."

"You need a plan."

My blood went cool at the words. What could I offer? "Are you going to help me with a plan?" I asked.

"Maybe."

"Do you try to fix all the strays you bring home?"

"I do what I can. Some make it. Some don't."

My heart hitched to hear him say it. The one whose room I had slept in last night hadn't made it. So far. Tarin had gone out of his way to try to find him. Had the two of them been closer than he was admitting?

Were there many others?

Was I next on his list of hopeless cases?

I wanted to be next on his list of successes. And maybe more. The same feeling and scent that had compelled me to follow him last night, beyond trying to get money from him, was there again, shivering my insides. Making me want to be the least hopeless one. The non-fuck-up.

"I know you said I'm not the type for this, but I am not a complete street brat. I am willing to work. I am willing to try."

"I didn't say you weren't the type for this sort of Omega rehab I do here."

"Right." I conceded. "You said I wasn't *your* type." I took a deep breath and felt his scent linger all over and inside me. Well, he was certainly my type. A strong disappointment washed over me that he didn't sense me that way in return.

When he did not reply to my statement, I bowed my head.

"Eat up." His voice trickled over me, a light caress. My imagination, of course. "Then I'll show you a few things. We'll talk more."

I wanted to talk more now, but he seemed firm about finishing the meal first.

Even if he didn't want me for some larger future, he was offering me a future nonetheless.

Seeing the other Omegas, the house, and his demeanor, I decided to trust him.

# Chapter Six

## *Tarin*

I wanted him. But I didn't take in lost Omegas to fuck them.

Kee had been one exception, but at the same time I took him in, I had never believed he could be more than the wild boy he was.

Alli was not like Kee at all. Yet something about Alli drew me, not innocence or virginity—I didn't need to be saddled with all that at my age. But there was a freshness to his eagerness, a sort of clean slate where things could be written, things I might want to read. Alli was the type who could be helped. But not if I allowed feelings to interrupt that.

I had to put all of that emotion off now that I'd decided Alli could stay and learn a trade. He would need focus to succeed. I'd already decided I would sponsor him. I would become his legal financial guardian. He did not need any distraction from that goal.

And neither did I.

But there was a tug in my mind from him, a pull. I need to ignore that.

I kept telling myself as a healthy Alpha I always felt that with Omegas anyway. I loved everything about them, their smaller, mostly hairless physiques, the need in their eyes, their intelligence that could complement an Alpha's if only they weren't so meek about it, so pushed back by society and its expectations of them.

So this pull toward Alli was perfectly natural. And for his own good, I simply needed to ignore it.

Kee had been one in a line-up of the hopeless that I'd had hope for only because I'd allowed my attraction to get out of hand. He was not the type, fit for the future I was offering, neither as a student or a lover.

But I'd been so blind to his charms.

Kee had laughed when I tried to create a contract between us; when I asked him about bondings and his feelings after some exquisite Burns we shared together.

Others before Kee, when I'd been very young, had also broken my heart.

I tried to choose my wards carefully. I'd made a lot of mistakes when I was younger. I thought I'd learned, until Kee came along. I'd slipped.

And now this one was making me feel out of control again. Maybe because I was still raw from Kee's absence. It had been months since I'd last seen him, but it felt like just yesterday he'd looked at me with his big green eyes through frazzled, dark hair and said, "I am not hanging for study group and you know it. Text me on your next Burn."

Now Alli stood in my office looking around at my set up, chewing on his lower lip and trying not to show how overwhelmed he was.

"You said last night," I began, "that you are turning eighteen today. This is your birthday, then."

"I forgot." His voice came out soft, contemplative, as if he could not believe it himself.

"Well, happy birthday. Hopefully, this will be a new start for you."

He bit back a smile. "Thank you."

"You know how to use a computer?"

He nodded. "The ones at the farm I learned on are old, but we got new ones recently."

"Good. If you want to stay and get a plan together for a possible future, let's start with some reading for you to do."

"Lessons?"

"Yes."

"In what?"

"Everything. Are you willing?"

He blinked at me. "Like a school?"

"Why not? What did you learn at the farm? Anything marketable?"

"I can take care of little ones. I can make a bed. I took a couple of cooking classes."

As usual. I sighed. Did Omegas learn science or math? Even literature? Not much, I knew. It was the way the world worked. But maybe Alli could learn.

I set him up to start off slow.

"You'll work in here today. But I will have a new computer set up in your room by tomorrow. That is where you'll work."

He nodded. "Yes, sir."

Already off to a good start.

"You'll have free time, of course. Television in the living room. There's also a game room. I suggest you get to know Oren, Farrell and Tev. They're older than you are, but very sociable and well-mannered."

"How long have they been with you?"

"Oren has been here a year now. Farrell and Tev, two years. They are about to both about to become licensed accountants. And Oren is studying to be a paralegal. There aren't many Omega accountants or paralegals, but it's a start."

"Then what will happen when they get licensed?"

"When they get work, they'll move out and get their own places and start to think about raising a family."

"But Tev and Farrell? I can tell they are a couple. Omega to Omega pairings produce monsters. Sylphs."

I nodded. "I will continue to be their guardian for their legal and financial matters, but beyond that, they will finally become independent and be able to be together as they've always wanted even if they have to pretend to be roommates only."

"Did you pick them to live here because they were lovers?"

"Yes. Otherwise, there was little hope for them in this world. And I chose them because I could tell they were determined to make it. I don't want to waste my time on lost causes."

Alli blanched a bit at my statement. "If I don't succeed, I'll—I'll try to find some way to pay you back."

"Why wouldn't you succeed?" I asked. "You have a healthy brain. You have a need to be on your own, away from the farm, for your own reasons. Is that not enough of a push for you?"

"It is, but I don't know how smart I really am."

"It's a matter of testing for your aptitudes. But that can come later. For now, I want you to read what I give you now."

"All right."

I left him to his reading for an hour and a half. Some light math problems and a short story.

When I came back, I gave him some tests to see if he'd done it all.

He passed. More than that, he got every question I put to him correct.

"Do you want more?" I asked.

He nodded. "I like the numbers when they make sense. But they're the hardest for me."

"If something doesn't make sense, you ask."

The tests I gave him were all rudimentary, but at least I could assess where he was on the learning scale.

Later in the morning, he asked, "Does this mean you're not kicking me out?"

"Maybe." I gave him a little wink before I realized he might see it as flirting.

His face flushed beautifully.

I needed to watch myself around this one. He was too easy on the eyes, and that scent—it was intoxicating.

He sat up a little straighter. "I'm afraid I'll mess up."

"Not to worry. You're doing fine."

I liked how he sat up; how he looked to me for more. It stirred me up again, and I clamped down hard on my response.

Later, after lunch, I gave him some free time and heard him go into the game room. I knew Oren was in there and I heard them talking. I wanted to spy, to see if they were getting along, but knowing Oren, everything was just fine.

I stayed away and went to my own room for a couple of hours where I had a second work computer.

That night, over dinner, which I had ordered in, Alli seemed more open and comfortable.

Oren and Alli were talking together as if they were old friends now. Oren was explaining how he loved organization and was really good at it.

Over pizza and hot wings, which all the boys loved, we made casual conversation.

Alli was quiet but relaxed, and he didn't eat too quickly, now. He was safe. For now he knew where his next meal was coming from.

When the feasting of hungry boys slowed, I brought out the cake.

Alli's eyes got very big.

"Why?" he asked.

"Why not?"

"You barely know me."

"It doesn't matter. I know it's your birthday. And I happen to like cake."

"How old are you today?" Oren asked.

"Eighteen."

"Just a baby." Farrell and Tev laughed, but their faces were kind.

Alli chewed on his lower lip. A habit he had, one I'd noticed throughout the day.

"Does this mean I'm staying for at least another night?" Alli asked.

"It does."

"But what about?" He stopped, glancing at Oren who shook his head.

"What about what?" I asked. I knew he wondered about the boy whose room he'd taken.

Alli shrugged.

I glanced about the table. "Kee isn't answering his texts and hasn't for weeks. He's not coming back. If he shows up, we'll deal with it."

The other boys all nodded.

"We're sorry," Oren said softly, looking up at me.

I took a deep breath. "It was expected, yes?"

Everyone agreed, the "yeses" going around the table.

I began to slice the cake into even pieces.

"What did they do for birthdays at your farm?" I asked Alli.

Alli's chest expanded as he prepared to answer. "We'd get cake, but only one piece. A lot of us shared birthdays. We'd get new uniforms. We'd get a ten dollar spending allowance online. We could buy a book or a beaded bracelet or something."

"Wow." I smiled, but that sort of treatment made me sad. Those boys—it didn't matter that they were Omegas— deserved better.

"It was the same where we were raised," Farrell said.

Tev nodded.

Oren said, "My parents used to go all out with the streamers and banners, all decorated with glitter." He did not elaborate further.

Alli said, "You're here, so they must not be around anymore?"

"Nope," was all Oren said.

Alli chewed his lower lip.

But when the cake was passed around to everyone, they were all smiles again, digging in to the sweet confection.

All in all, it had been a good day.

# Chapter Seven

*Alli*

It was both wonderful and frightening that Tarin was, so far, allowing me to stay. I had a whole room, a bed, and my own private bath. None of it felt like mine. Yet.

What if I failed him?

What Oren had told me in our afternoon together in the game room came back to me.

"You're in Kee's room, you know," Oren had said.

"Tarin mentioned there were clothes in the closet that belonged to another. I wasn't to touch them."

Oren's eyebrows had climbed high on his forehead. "I have to say I'm surprised he would bring you home and put you in there."

"Why? Hasn't this other Omega been gone for weeks?"

"Six months, actually. But Kee was special to Tarin. Even if he didn't live here full time, that room was sorta sacred. Tarin didn't want anyone else in there."

"They were lovers?" I had asked.

"Off and on, yes. Tarin's moodier when Kee is around, of course, but always sadder when he's gone. We all have a pact not to bring him up or say his name. It's best that way. So remember that. And don't ask him too many questions about Kee."

"All right. But what if—what if Kee comes back?"

Oren had shrugged. "At this point, he's been gone longer than ever. But if he does, I don't know."

"Will I be unwelcome?"

"No, nothing like that. Tarin brought you here. He has his reasons for that. Tarin wouldn't kick you out of the house, but maybe out of that room."

Oren had been easy to befriend, graciously answering all my questions.

Now I lay in Kee's bed looking around at an environment meant for another Omega. Tarin's Omega lover. I couldn't help but wonder what he'd been like. How they were with each other.

Oren said Kee had been disruptive. He wouldn't study. He would leave the house at all hours and not return for days. I could tell he was being polite, that there was more to Kee and his behavior than he was willing to admit.

Tarin had made it clear that he didn't sleep with his Omega guests, his wards. So why had he made an exception for Kee?

I searched the room but found nothing personal like photos or journals. Nothing but the clothes in the closet which Tarin had told me not to touch. I couldn't help but wonder what Kee looked like. And why did Tarin want him so?

I understood the reverse. Tarin was a powerful and large Alpha and he smelled exquisite. Any Omega would be attracted to him. I had been from the start even if I thought I'd only offer my body to him for money and be done. But I'd also followed him because he compelled me, whether he was conscious of it or not.

I couldn't help but lie still and listen for the sounds of him in the other room. One wall separated us. I heard the pipes when the water ran in his bathroom. I felt the slight tremble of the floor as he walked about getting ready for bed.

There was no scent of another Omega in this room. Obviously it had been thoroughly cleaned and cleared out, all except the clothes. Instead, I smelled only the soapy scent of polisher, and the air freshener labeled *apple spice* on the wall just inside the bathroom. But underneath all that, I breathed faint hints of autumn and vastness mixed with loneliness, and the atmosphere of newness mixed with old.

Tarin.

I had the impression Tarin had spent a lot of time in this room. With Kee. Maybe he came into the room to be closer to Kee when Kee was gone. Maybe he grieved him in here. But certainly, my senses were attuned enough to notice. He'd been here. Probably recently.

I closed my eyes and tried to fall asleep but I was too restless. I turned on the light and grabbed a tablet Tarin had loaned me, looking for something to read. But I couldn't concentrate.

I lay back against the soft pillows, considering how lucky I was. How easily I could still be out there freezing and starving on the streets, looking for any way to seek a warm bed and a meal just for one evening.

What had I done to deserve all this?

I heard some thumps in the room next door. Automatically, my mind went toward images of what he might be doing. Rearranging his covers. Moving toward his closet to disrobe.

My attraction to him resonated through me, especially now that I was quiet and in bed with the lights off and only my thoughts for company. I couldn't deny it when confronted with my own honest truths just before sleep. I wasn't only here because of the opportunity Tarin offered. Of course I wanted to better myself. But I wanted him.

It was stupid, I knew, to fall for the first Alpha I'd ever met. But he'd literally rescued me. Like in the perfect romance novel.

It saddened me because he showed no indication of wanting me in return. He was an altruist. That was what Oren had called him earlier today when we'd talked. I didn't really like that word because it meant, to me, that I wasn't all that special. That Tarin took me in out of pity and nothing more.

With those thoughts, as the sounds beyond the wall quieted, I entered a fitful sleep.

*

My second day at Tarin's house I showered, dressed and entered the hallway. It was still early but I was greeted by a stranger Omega who was vacuuming the long rug that ran from the staircase and past my and Tarin's rooms to the end of the hall.

He glanced up as I came out of the room, and smiled. "Hi." He turned off the vacuum. "I'm Enin."

"Alli," I replied.

"I expected you to be Kee."

"What?"

"I used to live here. You're in the room Kee used to stay in. I guess he's not here anymore."

I shook my head.

"Do you work for Tarin, then?" I asked.

"Well, right now. But actually I work for myself. I own a house cleaning business. I have six employees." He smiled, obviously proud of himself.

He was one of Tarin's graduates then, a success. Two days ago, I had never thought I'd be speaking with an Omega who owned his own business.

"Wow." I had no more words.

"Yeah. Tarin's great. You're one of the lucky few to be here. Congrats on being chosen."

"Thank you."

I wasn't sure if I was exactly chosen. Rather, I'd chosen Tarin. Pushed myself on him.

"So where's Kee? I'm assuming he's gone again. He was always that way," Enin said.

"I don't know. I never met him. I'm new. I think he's been gone for weeks, maybe longer."

"Too bad. Tarin really doted on him. I never understood it. Kee was such a fuck up." He reddened slightly. "I shouldn't have said that. He was a nice guy, really. Just not the teachable type."

A surge of jealousy pulsed through my veins. Stupid. I had nothing. I owned nothing. Tarin owed me nothing.

"Well," said Enin. "I should be getting back to work. We have another house after we finish here today. One of my crew will be up in a few minutes to change your sheets, clean your bathroom and do laundry. Did you make use of the laundry basket in your bathroom?"

I nodded, feeling strangely pampered and invaded at the same time. The luxuries of living with Tarin never seemed to end.

In the kitchen, at breakfast, Tarin presented me with my own laptop and a list of studies. I would no longer be on his computer in his office.

Already I felt cast out.

The computer was a wonderful gift. I could not dispute that. But it meant I would see less of Tarin and be more on my own.

When he set the laptop beside my breakfast plate, I wanted to reach out to him, not the gift. His hands were large and tan, the fingers strong and beautiful against the plastic computer case.

Tarin wore a dark blue button up shirt beneath a gray blazer. His black trousers fit him perfectly, with a slight crease at the crotch to accommodate his full maleness. That part of him was right at eye level from where I sat, and he stood so close to give me the gift that I smelled the freshness of the soap he'd used that morning, and the heady autumn night scent that catapulted my body and mind into a longing that almost hurt.

I had liked working in his office yesterday because I could be near his things, the essence of him. That office smelled like him.

Now I would be away from him. I would have no excuse to see him except at the end of the day to show him my completed assignments.

Hot pancakes dripping with butter and syrup sat on a plate before me, but that wasn't why my mouth watered.

"You can study anywhere you like with the laptop," Tarin said.

The unspoken part of that sentence was: *Just not in my office.*

"What if I need help? What if I have questions? Will I be able to come into your office?"

"Of course. I work away from home Tuesdays and Thursdays. I have a smart phone on order for you."

"A phone? Really?" I asked.

"Yeah." Oren pointed at me with his syrup-laden fork. "We just text him if we have questions that can't wait until the end of the day."

I half-resented Oren for speaking up, interrupting my time with Tarin. But it wasn't his fault I was such a ridiculous Omega who wanted the first Alpha he'd laid eyes on. I needed to get hold of myself. Yet, I didn't want to.

If that bully Gray had taught me anything, it was to stand up for myself, keep pushing. It got me punished in the past, but created a fire in me to not give up.

I looked away from Oren and back at Tarin's crotch, which was now, sadly, moving back and away from me.

I said, trying to keep Tarin from turning away, "It's too much, but thank you. You don't need to keep giving me expensive things."

"But you need them or you can't move forward with your life."

"His students pay him back if they can." Oren again. Interrupting again.

"I don't require it," Tarin said, ruffling Oren's pristine hair.

"The team cleaning the house here, right now, it's an Omega-owned business. Tarin set them up. They come in every week and clean the house for free." Oren looked pleased with himself for knowing and providing all this information.

"I met Enin," I said.

"I pay them," Tarin countered with a smile. "But they give me the family discount."

When Tarin smiled, his lips parted and his white teeth flashed. My neck muscles stiffened almost painfully as I gazed up at his face, the strong jaw, the dark bristle there from an unclose shave. It would feel rough and tingly on my fingertips, I decided. If could run my hands over and over that bristle, holding his face in place while I looked at him, sniffed him, tasted his plush pink lips—then I would be happy. Only then.

My face flushed at the thought.

Tarin didn't seem to notice. Oren snickered, and filled his mouth with big bites of pancake to cover it.

Tarin turned to the countertop, grabbed his keys which jingled against his palm, and said, "I'll be home at five, men. I expect you have to have your assignments done and be prepared to answer any questions. You have lunch fixings in the fridge. You get an hour. And you can take an hour in the afternoon for whatever."

The others all nodded knowingly. They'd been doing this for a while. Tarin turned and gave me a quizzical look, one eyebrow raised.

"Yes, sir." The reason I spoke aloud was because it seemed his words were for me and me alone.

I wanted to please Tarin. But also, I had thought when I reached the age of eighteen, my schooling would be over. I didn't hate school, but I had had a plan. To service Alphas in their Burns until I met the man of my dreams. We would then bond, marry and have a family.

Now the plan seemed to be "Let's find Alli work." That work was obviously and only something outside the sex trade. I wasn't ungrateful, but everything was new and strange, happening so fast. And I felt if I screwed it all up, I'd be out on my ass again.

I had to make this work. At the same time, I had to get control of my feelings. Tarin had made it clear he didn't want me.

If I didn't make myself work hard, he might toss me out and I'd be right back where I started. I'd have to go back to the Trenches and learn to sell myself. It was a hard life, but what other options did I have?

No, I had to make this student thing work with Tarin. I had to do well so he would keep me until I had skills enough to make it with him as my sponsor and guardian. I had to be like Enin and make my own business. Or like Oren, who was the epitome of the proper son, doing everything right and perfect. He'd be a great paralegal. He was perfect, polite and obedient. And those traits would certainly land him an Alpha mate as well, if that was what he aimed for.

I needed to do the same.

*

By afternoon, my frustration level had grown. The assignments were long and boring. Stuff about numbers which didn't make sense. Math. Science. Even boring literature—not the good stuff I liked like comics and sexy adventures. Tarin had assigned me stories to read that were all big words and awkward language, stuff about the old days I couldn't relate to, and one story was all about how the sun shone on a mountain range and made some guy lonely all the time until he stared too long into the sun and went blind. It was awful!

I confess, I scanned that one to the end.

By my break time, I had only completed half my math problems, and read very little of the science articles.

I explored the house a little, ending up in the game room.

Oren came in all energetic and happy.

"I finished my studies early for the day. You interested in a ping pong challenge?"

"Sure! I finished early, too!"

I was good at ping pong and I wanted to prove I could do something right. A lie like that could have gotten me the closet back at the farm. But I didn't want perfect Oren to upstage me, and who would know I hadn't finished my assignments? I'd catch up later this evening.

I beat Oren in every match. He won some games, but I won more, and by the time we were doused in sweat and laughing over missed serves, I saw it was five o'clock.

I pushed the damp hair from my eyes as I looked again at the clock to be sure I was seeing the numbers right. "Wow, we've been going at it for two hours."

"'I'm better at video games," Oren said. "But I'm at the computer too much. This was fun. But next time, I swear I'll beat you."

"Like hell."

"Have you seen the backyard yet?"

"No."

"Come on. Let's go out and cool off."

Oren led me down clean, sparkling hallways that smelled of lemon cleanser and to a room of windows. French doors opened onto a wide veranda with an oak deck, a wooden patio table and metal chairs, and a fountain. Beyond that, down a couple of cement steps, was a huge green yard of grass and trees. The grass was broken up with little patches of flowers and plants.

"We each have a garden," Oren pointed. "You can have one, too."

"I took a class in gardening," I said, feeling proud to be able to say so.

Oren took me on the backyard tour, pointing out the vegetable gardens, the flower gardens, and proudly naming each plant.

I nodded as if I knew their names, too, but in reality all I'd ever grown in gardening class back at Zilly's had been radishes and lettuce. And I had a potted ivy plant in my room. I knew little about flowers. At Zilly's, they wanted Omegas to learn about the pretty stuff to please their future Alphas, but I hadn't paid attention to that part of the class. I'd wanted to grow things I could eat. It seemed much cooler.

But that class had been over too soon and I'd never pursued gardening further.

I stood on the grass, breathing the fresh, flower-perfumed air and let the breeze cool the skin at my temples as it blew through my hair.

It really was wonderful here. I couldn't imagine going back to the Trenches now, even if my day had been somewhat frustrating. No way!

In that moment, I swore to myself I would double down on my studies and work twice as hard tomorrow.

# Chapter Eight

*Tarin*

Alli sat before me in the chair beside my desk as I looked through his work for the day. He was silent, looking at his knees, strands of his brown hair falling forward to shadow his cheeks.

"Did you not understand the math explanation here on page six?" I asked.

"Sort of."

"Sort of? You didn't finish the homework problems. And what you did do, well, a lot of your answers are incorrect."

Alli's hands folded together in his lap. He pressed down hard until his knuckles were white. "They are?"

"Yes. This one has to be done over, I'm afraid. Do you have questions? I can answer them."

He shook his head.

"If you don't understand this, I can help."

"I was just distracted. That's it. I think my mind wanders or something."

"Did you have this problem in your classes at the farm?"

"Sometimes. I guess." He shrugged.

His entire demeanor seemed shut down.

"And this worksheet here, for general introduction to science. You didn't complete it."

"I didn't finish the chapter."

"Okay. Did I give you too much to do?"

"Maybe." Now he looked up and his face seemed pale.

"Did you read the two stories I assigned?"

He nodded. "Well, I scanned the first one. It was boring. The second one was worse."

"Then you didn't really read them."

He did not reply.

I stared at the assignments for a moment. They weren't difficult. Everything was high school level introductory. "I'm not sure what to do here."

Alli gripped his hands harder and seemed to shiver once. His voice came out low. "I promise I'll work harder. What are you going to do to me now?"

"Do to you?"

"For not completing the assignments."

I frowned. "Do you mean something like a punishment?"

The boy's eyelids lowered as he nodded once. A glimmer sparked behind them. Were those tears? Something in my chest fluttered.

"I don't punish anyone here."

"But surely if someone doesn't work out here, you don't let them stay."

"That's never happened."

"Never?" His sleek eyebrows went up.

"But I suppose there are always firsts. If someone committed a crime, or tried to harm one of the others here, then I'd have to do something. You don't strike me as the violent type. Or a criminal. Even if you might have been thinking of taking what was in my pocket the first night we met."

"No, sir. I'd never want to hurt another."

"There are always different paths for different people. Not everyone is cut out to be an engineer like me. Or run a housekeeping business like Enin. Everyone's different. All I want to see is that you are trying."

"I'll re-do the assignments." His eyes began to glow as if with a renewed determination, the lashes glossy in the desk's light as he blinked. "I'll try harder tomorrow, I promise."

"Good."

"I like to read but I didn't like these stories." Alli pointed at the screen to the book title I'd assigned him.

"What do you like?"

"Manga. Comics."

"Of course." He was young. It was a given he wanted those sorts of books.

"Novels with adventure and maybe some sexy times," he added.

"I'll tell you what. You read one short story out of here a day and then the rest of your reading can be a novel a week of your choice. Not a comic book. Okay? Then I want a review of each. No less than two-hundred and fifty words."

"I can do that."

"I understand it will take time to settle in." I paused, worried I had thrust him into this too quickly. He had only just become an adult. He had been only days away from the farm, the only place he'd ever known as a home in his short life.

I wanted to reach out to him, touch him, reassure him. He was safe here. No one would punish him. No one was going to throw him out, least of all me.

I didn't do physical contact with my Omega guests, my students. Brief handshakes, a gentle hand on a shoulder, and that was about it.

I thought again of Kee, but he didn't count.

I had hoped, of course, Kee could be rehabilitated, and maybe eventually want to bond with me. But he'd only ended up being a disruptive influence on the others, and turning a cool eye to my greater affections. I'd never thrown him out. He'd always left on his own and without warning.

Alli was not like Kee at all. He was younger, less experienced, soft not loud, innocent not hard. His build, his coloring—everything was different. A beautiful boy.

Alli made me think things I didn't want to deal with. I kept telling myself he wasn't what I wanted, but that was a lie. I couldn't stop thinking about him—all day at work. And now, with his frustrations and damp anxieties of youth squirming to please me. He'd said he wanted me. The prettiness of him, his youth, his scent which created a strange pain deep in my chest, like heat and cold mixing. He was magnetic in ways I couldn't deny.

A small voice broke me out of my thoughts.

"Sir?"

"Yes?"

"Maybe if I work tonight before bedtime on all this, I can catch up. I can try."

"No. You're going to come into the living room with the rest of us and watch a movie. It's a movie a night. That's what we do here to decompress. If you work all the time, you will burn out and we can't have that can we?"

He shook his head and his hair fell back. His sweet eyes seemed to grow bigger and rounder.

"We'll have popcorn and it'll be fun."

"But I don't think I deserve—"

"You're not allowed to think that way," I interrupted. "What every person deserves is decency from others and a chance. A chance to strive. You'll do better tomorrow, right?"

He nodded.

"Good."

It shouldn't have been big eyes and all innocence that drew me, but it did. The fact that he'd shown little interest in his learning should have exasperated me. Instead, I wanted to comfort him even more. I realized he hadn't had time to acclimate, and my thoughts kept clamoring to make excuses for him.

Why did I just want to hug him? Hold him?

I treated my Omega guests well, but I didn't coddle them in that way. And Kee, well, he wouldn't allow coddling even if I'd wanted it. Even if I'd wanted to hold him in my arms after crazed Burn sex and breathe in his scent. No, he wouldn't have it, and I had worked to close that foolish part of myself off.

Until Alli.

Something had awakened inside me, but so soon after Kee, I had to tamp it down because this could not be happening. Not so fast. Not so strong.

But those big eyes shone, darkly expressive. Did he even understand his unique allure?

His focus zoomed in on me as if I owned the world. All my other Omega boys, the ones I'd taught, the ones I'd sponsored and maintained guardianships with didn't affect me in this way.

I stood and stretched, making my way to the door. Alli followed.

In the living room, Farrell and Tev were already curled up together on the loveseat. Oren sat in a recliner with an iced soft drink in hand. A large bowl of popcorn occupied the center portion of the coffee table, but the boys had little bowls of it on their laps.

"The movie's all set up." Oren brandished the remote.

"He won't give up that remote," Tev said.

Farrell laughed. "Pretending you're the Alpha of the house, Oren?"

Oren made a face at him.

Alli trailed behind me. I took a chair for myself. Alli looked around for a place to sit. He could have used any number of other chairs, but instead he plopped on the ground near my chair.

My heart flopped in my chest. He obviously wanted to sit with me.

Oren got up and handed both of us small bowls filled with popcorn. "The fridge is full of drinks," he said to Alli.

Alli nodded. "Okay. Thanks."

The lilt of Alli's young voice thrummed through me.

Oren started the movie, one they'd all picked out beforehand. I didn't ask the title. I didn't care. This was their time to relax and reward themselves. To spend time together. Sometimes I didn't stay long, letting them have the room, letting them be together as Omegas without the influence of an Alpha around.

But tonight I stayed. I wasn't watching the movie. My senses were overloaded with Alli, fragrance of white hot roses, attar of summer, elegant and rainy Aprils reminding me when I was kid dreaming on my front porch, playing in bright endless afternoons before I knew what Alphas and Omegas were to each other, and believing I would one day own the world. That young me, with no concerns but lining up my toy cars and catching butterflies on the wind made me half-shut my eyelids. I saw him as a tousled kid full of smiles.

My reverie deepened.

As I had grown older, leaving childhood behind, the interruption of adolescent pangs and pains had worried me more than I'd let on to my Alpha and Omega parents. I loved them both equally but when I discovered Omegas had less options for their own futures, and Omega chattel were used to service Alpha Burns, I had nightmares. I wondered how one-half of the population could be treated as if—as if they were slaves.

I found a group of chaste Alphas online who discussed the same concerns. Many weathered their Burns alone, and had advice on sex aids and toys for cooling the Burn without paying for Omega partners.

I tried celibacy during my Burns a few times, but I had hated it. My Omega father was the one who convinced me I wasn't immoral for using Omega farms. It was the way he and my Alpha dad had met.

Now in my early fifties, still young for an Alpha, I remained single. I'd had very few love affairs in my life. And none that panned out to more.

My gaze remained fixed on Alli, the movie going on unnoticed, background noise only to my thoughts.

Already I'd fantasized about Alli naked, and felt things I wasn't expecting to experience from a youngster I barely knew.

The movie blared.

The boys laughed.

Once Alli turned to me and said, "Oh gods. Wow!" He was grinning.

I had no idea what he was reacting to on the screen. I merely smiled back, nodding.

"You've seen this before," he accused.

Honestly, I had no idea if I had or not. Whatever they were watching, I had paid it no attention. I shrugged.

Oren frowned. "It's brand new."

"Shut up," said Tev.

"Run it back a few seconds," Farrell demanded.

My popcorn lay in my lap untouched.

When the movie ended, I couldn't have told anyone what we'd just watched. The genre might have been action/adventure, but I couldn't be sure.

Turning in for the night, I wasn't the least bit tired.

Every moment in my bed was me struggling with my body to find a comfortable position. Nothing seemed right. I tossed and turned. I took my temperature to see if I had an early onset of the Burn. I was normal.

I listened intently if I heard any creak or rustle through the walls in the room next to mine, Kee's room. I imagined Alli in there moving around, stripping naked, getting ready for bed. I imagined him lying under cool white sheets, his body gleaming in the faint pale light from the night light in the bathroom. His body brushed with shadow and crisp linen. His body young and untouched, his yearning gaze staring upward.

Was he unable to sleep as well?

I decided I should have put him in a room downstairs, and moved Oren into Kee's room. I had no designs on Oren, or any of the others I'd brought into my home over the years. I chose them for their neediness, or if they found me first, and I had room, I acquiesced to their needs, but I never had attraction.

They were house-mates. Even when I had my Burns every two months, I didn't think about them. I didn't have designs on them. I moved out for two or three days. I sought chattel.

Alli, though, made me suddenly question everything. He smelled too good. He made me think of my childhood. He made my insides tighten.

After I'd treated him to his burger dinner, which he had not kept down, I should never have brought him home.

And yet, guilt at that very thought pestered me, because he deserved as much of a chance as Oren, Tev and Farrell. And the others. I had said it to him. *Everyone deserves decency and a chance.* He deserved space here as much as any, as much as even Kee.

It was all my fault I was feeling this way. I hadn't properly seen to my needs outside the Burns to maintain control. Kee had messed me up. My fault, again, for falling for that wild boy. My fault all the way.

I had unrealistic expectations. I had needs I denied until they got out of control.

When would I learn?

I had to be firm with myself. I would not allow these feelings for Alli to control me. I would not fall for the wrong boy again.

*

"I made up my time on all of it," Alli said proudly, showing me his homework.

It was his second day of studies, his third day in my home.

I sat quietly, going over his math. Nearly every problem. Wrong. Wrong. Wrong.

But he'd tried.

He got up and looked over my shoulder and I really didn't want him that close to me. It was too nice and I needed to remember my decision to be firm. To not respond to him and drive myself into insomnia yet again tonight.

"Those are wrong?" He pointed at my big desk screen.

"Yes. You got those two right, though."

His eyes down-turned. "Wait. All the rest of them are wrong?"

"I'm afraid so." I didn't want to tell him, to dissuade him. This Omega had a gentle soul. He'd been through abuse from the farm, and threats to institutionalize him. I didn't want him to believe the decision of his abuser to send him away as unworthy could ever be true.

"You tried hard. I can see your work. But on this problem, here, you didn't carry the one. See?"

"Oh. Such a stupid mistake. I see."

"And here." I showed him more of what he'd done wrong.

"I thought I was being careful." There was a sinking tone in those words. "I don't know why I didn't see. I'm pretty stupid, I guess."

"I won't hear that, all right?" I turned to him. "That word is not allowed."

"If it's true—" He pouted, and took a deep, hissing breath through his nose.

"I can show you some things that will be helpful."

"Okay." His look changed immediately to one of hope again. I liked to see it. I didn't want him unhappy here.

We spent the next two hours going over many things, including the science questions, many of which he'd also gotten wrong... or almost right.

Technically, he'd failed again, but I would never lead him down that road of thinking it. No one failed who tried, and tried again.

We talked of the story he'd read that afternoon and which he, again, hated, and of the novel he'd chosen to read for the week. He seemed a little more on board with literature than the other subjects.

When he glanced at my desk clock, his eyebrows shot up. "Wow, it's late! I didn't mean to keep you so long from your work."

"It's all right." Honestly, I hadn't noticed the time. Just like last evening with the movie, I hadn't cared about that part of it. It was as if spending time in the presence of Alli made everything else disappear.

*No.* I couldn't think that way. I had to be firm.

"But you have your own work. And you said before that evenings were for relaxing. And we've been working."

"There are exceptions to my rules all the time."

Alli raised a young and delicate, untouched eyebrow at me. My chest flooded with warmth.

"I think I made you up," he said softly.

"What?"

"One of my childhood teachers used to say, 'If it seems too good to be true, it's probably not true.' I guess he was trying to make us not so gullible or something. And to prepare us for a world at large that make Omegas vulnerable because we're more submissive."

"Good and bad happens all the time in this world," I replied. "Your teacher was right, but in a very general way. He was probably trying to instill in you some common sense. That you shouldn't simply believe everything you're told without some investigation first."

"Right. Don't just accept things at face value. Use your mind." He tapped the side of his pretty head.

"Exactly."

I knew I was doing a good thing here. A rare thing. Helping Omegas.

But did that make me good?

Alli gave me a sheepish smile. "Maybe I also need to learn to take the hand up when it is given, and not question it so much."

"Of course you should question. Always. Questioning should not be something to be avoided. You can only grow and learn and become your best self if you keep questioning."

"Can I ask you something then?"

I nodded.

"Why do you do this?"

I shrugged. "Because I can."

"But, but... All right. You said to question. I will, then. This can't be it. You teaching me. Me living here. I don't understand. I'm taking up your time. I—I don't know how to ask, but I keep wondering. When you have your Burn, I mean, it's all I have to give in return. All--"

I held up my hand for him to be quiet. "I told you I don't sleep with my house-guests."

"I don't know about the others, but I was farm trained. For servicing Alphas. It's what I know how to do. Enin pays you back by cleaning your house. Some day Oren will make a lot of money and pay you back in that way. But I keep wondering about me. What I can do. And clearly I'm not smart." His voice softened as if he became suddenly shy. "But I am service-trained. I can pay you back in that way."

A yearning tug. A gravity. Like stars.

I needed to be firmer. I would not repeat the mistakes I'd made with Kee.

"No," I said.

Alli's whole body slumped. His face darkened with a flush and my body responded to that with its own rush of unexpected heat. I clamped down on it, exercising firm control.

Emotions tangled up everything. I wanted Alli to succeed. I had made my promise to him. I wanted to keep it. No other distraction. When I committed to a boy, I committed all the way. To his future. To my guardianship of that.

If I kept emotion away, all would be well. My affection for the boy could not be undone. The responsibility had already infused in me a clenching need to do right by him. But the other need, the one that forced him upon my thoughts all hours of the day and night, that I didn't promise to anyone. Not even to myself.

I need not listen to my inner thoughts. Or my fantasies. I was mature. Adult. I could control myself around Omegas.

Alli was no different from the rest. If I took advantage of him, it would be wrong.

I told myself this again and again. For all the good it might do.

"Do not concern yourself for one moment about paying me back," I said. "Put it out of your mind."

"But, sir--"

"No. I won't hear of it."

"But what if I wanted to. Just me. Because I felt it, wanted it." His lashes caught and seemed to reflect the amber light of the overhead fixture.

Dear gods. I had to quash this now.

"I told you when we met. You're not my type."

# Chapter Nine

## *Alli*

I wasn't his type.

I looked in the mirror, flicked back my hair, which was glossy and pretty and, well, nicely framed my face if I did say so myself. I had a lean body, slim hips, a tight and nicely rounded ass. The kind I was taught Alphas liked. Friends told me I'd do well in the mating hall when I came of age.

Tarin had said when we first met he didn't like virgins. It would take too much effort.

Scenarios ran through my mind, arguing with the Alpha. "I'm trained. I'll be no effort at all!" was always my final statement, confirming to him he was wrong.

But everything about this evening—from getting my math problems wrong, and not understanding general science, to Tarin putting off my offer to service his Burn—had gone wrong. My offer had been appropriate and above-board. Polite and proper. He had a need. I could fulfill it. And I wanted him. Of my own accord.

So why did I feel like the filthiest eighteen year old this side of the Trenches?

It was because of my feelings. I knew it. And because of how he smelled and looked and sounded. Because of his generosity. He truly wanted good things for me.

All that only made me want him more. How could Oren not feel it, too? Maybe he had different tastes. Tev and Farrell only had the ability to focus on each other, so I understood their indifference to the magnificent Alpha who daily graced their presence.

But for me, I couldn't figure out up from down half the day. Maybe that was why I'd gotten so much of my homework wrong.

There wasn't a place in the house I could go that I did not scent Tarin's essence, even when he wasn't home. Only my room seemed somewhat free of his uniquely Alpha perfume after Enin's crew had cleaned it. I loved that room, but I hated it, too. It had belonged to Tarin's lover, Kee.

While I couldn't sense or smell Kee, knowing it had been his room left me slightly resentful.

There weren't even any photos of Kee around. So I couldn't see how I might compare in the looks department. Part of me didn't ever want to know.

Because I couldn't sense Tarin in that room, now, I wanted to leave it often. Except at night when I knew he was right next door. Then everything was perfect. I could strain my ears to try to hear him walk about, shuffle his feet on the floor, shower, change his clothes. That was all good—when I felt him close. Closest. At night.

And then I was glad I had that room. Happy to be upstairs with Tarin, alone, and not in the downstairs section with the other Omegas.

It had been all about timing, and not about me being anyone special, that gave me this room. But I liked to think otherwise late at night, just before sleep. That somehow I *was* special. And maybe, just maybe I was on Tarin's mind the way he had invaded mine.

*

I gave a groan as I hurled the book across the room.

I had read the math chapter three times and it still didn't make sense.

I couldn't focus on the science.

And the novel I'd chosen for the week had gotten boring.

Oren sat on a plush, red velvet couch playing video games when I entered the game room.

"You're finished early," he said without looking up from the TV.

I plopped down next to him on the couch and leaned my head back staring at the ceiling.

"I feel like it's going to take me forever to learn anything. And then, what will I do with the knowledge?"

"You'll figure it out. Give yourself time. This is only your third day."

"How long have you been here?" I asked.

"It will be a year next month."

"A year?"

"I'm taking some very difficult online classes. There's a lot involved with becoming a paralegal."

"That's like being a lawyer, right?"

"Not quite, but almost. My classes are high level and I'm getting a degree as well. I study fast. I learn fast. But it might mean another year here even with all that."

He gave a yell and I jumped forward, startled, only to see him crash and burn, the *GAME OVER* icon flashing in the middle of the screen.

He turned to face me. "You can't be impatient with yourself. Most Alphas take four years to get through a full college education. Trade schools are anywhere from six months to two years. With Tarin tutoring us, we can move faster, but we still go at the pace that we choose. Whatever's comfortable for us."

I sighed. "I feel so dumb. I'm taking classes that are high school level still."

"You'll get there."

"But I don't even understand them!" My fist hit the arm of the couch.

"You can text Tarin any questions you have."

"I know. I haven't, though. I feel awkward interrupting him even when he's home." My whole body quivered when I was around Tarin. The thought of texting him, strangely, made me go hot and cold at the same time.

Oren laughed.

"Hey, don't laugh at me."

"Sorry. I remember when I first came here. I was shy and scared. My parents both died in a car crash."

"Sorry. I can't even imagine how that would feel. I've never known my parents."

"I was devastated. I was eighteen, too old to go to a farm or a foster home. They left me money, though. Because of my grades, and my high marks on intelligence tests, my Alpha dad had actually wanted to send me to an exclusive Omega college. But I couldn't legally get access to the money and so even though I'd been accepted to the college, there was no way I could go. My Alpha grandfather had other ideas. He decided to put a hold on the money until I married, which made no sense because I had nothing to live on until I found someone. Then he set me up to marry an Alpha in another country. I found out he was selling me. Getting rid of me and getting paid at the same time. He tried to lock me away. I ran and Tarin found me. I was lucky."

"I ran, too."

"From Zilly's, right? Tarin told us a little about you. But Zilly's has a pretty good rep, I've heard."

"Not if you have one crazy pervy house-dad out to get you and no one believes you. He was going to institutionalize me because I witnessed him rape a student."

"Wow. Tarin knows this?"

"Yeah."

"You're safe here, you know. Tarin would never hurt any Omega."

I scratched my fingers hard across the velvet of the couch arm. "Tarin's the first Alpha I've ever met."

"Yeah? You never saw any who came to the farm?" Oren asked.

"Usually they come to service their Burns. The mating hall is a separate building from where we live."

Oren's face flushed starting at the temples and moving down to his jaw. "I've never been to any farms. I wasn't sure."

"We're raised to perform that duty. It's considered an honor."

"I lived pretty sheltered. I was a mess when Tarin found me. Sex wasn't my talent, or in my thoughts. But the streets were only about that. Or dealing. I'm not an Omega-lover like Farrell and Tev, but I didn't think about it much so I was pretty naive. I figured I'd meet an Alpha much later in life. If ever. When Tarin took me in, I thought I was dreaming. I thought I had died and this was my mind's last fantasy. Because everything else was hell for me. Utter hell."

I liked Oren. He made me feel like I wasn't such a misfit.

"Give yourself time," Oren said. "It's a safe place here. For now, that's all you need to know. And Tarin is happy, as long as he sees all of us are trying."

I didn't dare tell Oren my deepest secret, that I wanted Tarin. That my training had set me up to crave Alphas, and if one was going into the Burn, offering myself was the right thing to do.

But more, Tarin's presence made my entire body light up.

Only three days and I wanted more, both from myself and from Tarin.

Oren was right when he said I should give it time. I'd learn to fit in. But I didn't need time. I wanted Tarin. And the specter of Kee made me feel more urgent. That somehow I needed to compete. I needed to be the best.

But how could I be the best if I couldn't even complete a homework assignment without getting everything wrong?

On top of that, I feared Tarin would tire of me after a while, after having to go over every assignment with me ten times before I understood.

76

That would not do.

Later in the afternoon, Oren and I put on jeans—new ones had been delivered to me that day—and went into the gardens. The sunlight and the green grass and the scent of growing things bought me solace, and before I knew it several hours had passed. My hands and new jeans were dirty from pulling weeds, watering, and picking ripe vegetables and putting them in baskets.

Though I grew up on a farm, it wasn't *that* kind of farm where we grew food and harvested it.

Oren always seemed so right and proper in the house, clothes clean and ironed, pale hair perfect, his chin held high and proud. But outside he became another man. He let his shirt hang open. He laughed more. He didn't seem to mind the dirt.

I was glad he'd told me about his life, and how he wasn't interested in Alphas yet. I wanted him for a friend, not competition. But I kept wondering, if he knew my secret thoughts, would he disapprove? Would he despise me for being more visceral, less intellectual? Would he think I was an idiot for developing feelings for the first Alpha I'd ever met?

Farrell came out and called us to dinner. It was then I realized I hadn't finished my assignments again. I had spent hours outside with Oren.

At least I'd enjoyed myself.

\*

Though Tarin had said he didn't toss Omegas into the street for not doing their homework, I wasn't sure I completely believed him.

All through dinner, the guilt ate at me. I said nothing, but as I pushed my food around on my plate, I would not look at Tarin, who sat perfectly groomed and at ease, whose aura filled the space around us with confidence and security. *Security for those who've earned it.* His presence shouted to all my senses, as if the room overflowed with him because he was so big, because he fairly throbbed with Alpha energy.

My veins throbbed to sense him near me. My mouth went dry no matter how much water I drank.

Why didn't the others feel this way? Why was it only me?

And Tarin, well, he acted closed off, unreadable, and remained soft-spoken and polite and calm throughout the dinner. As if four Omegas in the same room with him didn't affect him. As if we were ordinary people just like him.

I dreaded the moment he would see me in his office to discuss my day's work. I was always the last one called in. Oren was always first. Oren never took more than five minutes alone with Tarin because he was so smart. Because all his work was done perfectly, I presumed.

Farrell and Tev also never seemed to make trouble. They stayed to themselves, quiet and quietly involved in each other when not studying. They often took off on walks, or drives in the car Tarin had provided for all of us to share.

I didn't know how to drive yet, so I didn't have my own set of keys. But Oren assured me driving would become a part of my lesson plans as well.

I waited in the gleaming hallway. The sun had set, so the far window at the end of the hall was dark, the teal curtains pulled back to reveal shadow upon shadow. I still couldn't believe I was really off the streets and living here. As if I were in some kind dream.

I decided to be brave as I waited for Tarin to see me. I would not feel guilt. I would keep my head up and tell Tarin what I wanted. What I needed. I simply wasn't cut out for science or math. I wanted to please Tarin, because those were the subjects he thought of as important, but I couldn't focus.

And my crush on him wasn't helping matters any, either.

Finally, Tarin called me into his office.

I walked in with my laptop and some paper notebooks I was using as worksheets.

"Hello, Alli, how was today? You were pretty quiet at dinner." His voice washed over me with a kind of echoing cadence that seemed to infuse itself into my very pores. To anyone else, it might be a casual communication.

I could barely look at him without feeling my body tremble. From the moment I followed him on the street to now, things had only gotten worse in that respect.

There was that sensation again of an oncoming October night and a secret power behind it, a scent mixed with wood-fire and dry leaves. He was like a hot cup of tea, my mouth watering.

Tarin didn't realize, of course, that with his every gesture—pushing his hair back from his tall, tan forehead, raising his arm with the shirt cuff rolled up to expose his skin and the underside of his elbow, leaning his tall body back in his chair so that its wheels creaked on the mat underneath it—he was causing parts of me to dissolve and drift away, my mind a tangle, my bones a jumble.

He reached for my work books. I dropped one as I handed them to him. One of the books was bent wrong, the back cover folded to a crease.

I leaned over to pick up the fallen book.

"What happened?" he asked, looking at their state.

"I'm sorry." What was this? Me apologizing again. Fear came up to consume me when I knew he wasn't going to do anything terrible. Somehow, though, my body didn't know that. My body didn't know anything, or obey simple commands, it seemed. One minute it was melty and full of longing and the next it was pulling back, cringing at my guilt, anticipating the closet or the paddle which Gray had wielded until it left bruises.

Tarin wouldn't do that.

"Sit, Alli," Tarin said, indicating the chair next to him.

I plunked myself down, staring at my closed computer in my lap.

"Did you drop this one before now?" Tarin asked, holding up the creased and damaged workbook.

I took a deep breath. "I threw it across the room."

"You threw--?"

I forced myself to look him in the eye. I'd done it with Gray many times, made myself face him and not look away. But I didn't feel the same as I did now. For one, I hated Gray. I didn't care what he did. But Tarin—I liked him very much. I cared too much. About what he would think. Do. Say.

Without another word, Tarin opened the workbooks. Then he opened some windows on his computer and read for a while. All my assignments were open for him to see on his computer.

"I see," he said. "You're having trouble with science. And math. An—"

"Everything!" I blurted.

He looked at me with keen blue eyes and the color in them seemed to shift dark to light to dark with his unspoken thoughts.

He frowned at me. "You are still doing sloppy work."

I bit hard on my lower lip.

"I know you're still settling in," said Tarin.

"I'm stupid, that's it."

"What did I say about that word?"

"Not to use it," I answered.

"You do want to be here, do you not?"

"Yes." I blinked as hotness began to seep through my eyes.

"What did you do today? Not your studies, that's a given."

"The garden." I swallowed. "I like it outside."

Tarin leaned forward in his desk chair. "Ah, Oren mentioned you helped him bring in all those fresh veggies we had in our salads tonight."

"I spent the entire afternoon out there," I said. "I'm sorry."

"Don't be sorry. You're very young. You're still finding yourself."

*Young.* It sounded like a crime. And maybe it was. Oren was older by only two years but it felt like leaps and bounds.

The room seemed to close in on me, the walls with all their pretty pictures of mountains and seascapes, the floor patterned with ornate rugs, and even my chair. Too small, too confining, and too close to Tarin. His warmth intruded over me. Around me. It was as if we were already touching and yet still inches away from each other.

Tarin raised his eyebrows, then shifted as if uncomfortable. His chair squeaked and he leaned toward his computer again.

The air seemed hot now. Did he feel it, too?

"Everything in your life has been disrupted." He didn't wait for an answer from me, or even seem to want an explanation of my own feelings. "How about lighter reading for a while, and I'm going to give you something else. Open your computer."

With shaky hands I lifted the lid and turned it on. My unfinished assigned readings stared me in the face. Boring. Hard. Making me feel like an ungrateful brat. I should have been able to do this. It should have been easy.

Then something popped in live on my screen. Two books. On gardening.

"These may be more to your liking. A chapter a day. I want you to make your own projects as homework. Clear some space in one or two of the garden beds for yourself."

I glanced up, blinking hard. "Really?"

If Tarin thought this was punishment for me, he was crazy.

"Really." The hint of a smile dusted his face.

I sucked on the insides of my cheeks to keep my excitement from overwhelming me.

"That's all," he said lightly, turning back to his screen.

I was dismissed too soon. I hadn't had the proper chance to tell him all my thoughts. And maybe some of my secrets. Maybe *all* of my secrets.

"Sir. Tarin." I stood, closing my laptop and holding it against my chest.

"What?"

"I—I feel like I've done so much wrong."

He looked up, lips parting, pink, perfect. "You haven't done anything wrong."

How I wanted him to like me. Need me the way I needed him. I could toss and turn all night and to no avail. He could go into the Burn tomorrow and simply leave the house for three days.

"I can do more than gardening." My voice came out too high, too unsure. I shook it off, straightening my shoulders. "Again, I just want to say my services, my offer—it's still open."

His gaze seemed to unfocus, his body go tight. "So you've told me. Is that all?" He turned as if to dismiss me again.

I stayed standing where I was. "I know, but, just so you know. Nothing has changed."

He held up his hand to stop me, but it wasn't mean or firm. His palm faced the floor. "No need. You can go now."

I tilted back, head up. "I want to!" I blurted.

He looked up at me and his blue eyes glistened. Was he bored or interested?

"It's all I know. It's what I was trained for. And my stupid house-dad wrecked everything." I hugged my laptop tighter to my chest. "You're the first Alpha I've met. Ever. I know I must look stupid to you. A child." I needed to stop myself. Now. But my lips kept moving and words kept coming out of my mouth. "But I—it's all I had in my life. It was my goal. To work the mating hall, find an Alpha and bond." I felt the muscles around my lips tighten into an unruly pout.

Shame rushed over me, heating my cheeks.

Tarin's gaze remained flat. His body stiff. Unmoving. Finally, he placed his hand on his desk and leaned into it. "You have a lot of time here to figure things out. Do not rush it."

Rush what? I wanted Tarin now!

I tried hard to relax my immature pout.

"You can't do everything. Not all in one day," Tarin added.

What did he mean by everything? Surely not my offer. All he did was decline me.

My heart slowed and my insides felt scrambled, my mind whirling in a sensation of falling. I blinked, unable to look away. Who could ever look at Tarin's smooth face, his five o'clock shadow—something most Omegas didn't have— his broad shoulders, the way he held himself secure and unafraid as if he owned the world, and not crave it? Everything in me leaned toward him.

But it was foolish to want what didn't want you back. *If it's too good to be true--*

I turned away from him and it hurt to no longer see the angles of his body and the glow of his dark hair, and how the light shaded and enhanced the folds and valleys of his clothing, and the planes of his beautiful face. The scent of him—wild winds and secret nights—didn't change but only increased, which confused me even more. The ache in me increased like nothing I'd ever felt. But obviously, Tarin didn't feel it in return.

Such a fool I was!

I scurried to the door, flinging it open, exiting his office at a run. I went so fast my footsteps on the rug and then the marble tile barely registered, echoing far behind me as I ran, still clutching my laptop, past the kitchen.

No one was about.

I made it to the French doors at the back of the house that led to the veranda, pushing them open and letting myself go, computer still hugged to me as I ran down the stone stops and onto the dew-damp grass.

It was cool outside. A half-moon shone through the branches of neighboring trees. The garden beds actually glowed, as if life itself produced a visible, faintly blue aura in the darkness.

I moved through the dampness and let the wind softly wash my face with its cool breath.

I quickly strolled past sleeping flowers and the dark shadows of vines and plants to the garden I'd worked in most of the day. Wicker baskets sat in a line along the edge of the bed waiting for more harvest. Everything smelled liquid and clean, slightly minty.

I knelt in the grass, the knees of my trousers instantly soaked, and I took huge gulps of the night-damp air.

Outside in this beautiful yard all was peaceful and calm. My heart had been revved up the whole time I'd been in Tarin's office, despite its fall of disappointment in both my own bluster of words to Tarin, and Tarin's response.

After a few minutes, it resumed a sturdy, healthy beat. My limbs stopped shaking. They were shaking? I hadn't noticed until they calmed. Until my muscles softened and my mind's thoughts slowed to a safe cadence.

The dark song of crickets surrounded me. Leaves whispered in the faraway trees. Wisdoms. Comforts.

My computer tilted on my lap as I sat my butt against my calves and heels, trying not to get the seat of my pants wet, trying to relax more.

All the jumbles of my life went away in this yard, in the darkness, in the feel of nature all around me—nature as intended. Things were clear-cut. Even if in the wild animal life fought for food, for territory, for mates, it was cut and dry, with no worrying involved. What happened happened fast and furious without question in the wild.

Animals didn't spend a lot of time worrying about it all, fretting, suffering. Plants especially took their natural courses with elegance and grace and not too much fighting among themselves unless the weeds took over to choke them, and even then, the weeds themselves were only doing as they were willed to do to thrive.

For a long time I sat, listening to the night sounds, the peace of it all, the unending course and throb of life.

In my bones, young and needy and unsatisfied, a virgin man on the cusp of new adulthood, ready and wanting but with no experience, and with confines and dictates of being farm-raised influencing my every move, I could feel the call of my kind—the Alpha I wanted. The first Alpha I had ever met.

It might have been foolish, but the feelings were real. I knew they were. The strength of them cut to my core. How could this pain not reflect a real, honest desire? Deep in my bones, I couldn't deny the truth.

I wanted Tarin. I wanted it all. Omega-brat, that I was. Shaped by a sheltered life and a scary, pervert house-dad.

I wanted what I wanted and that couldn't be helped.

But if Tarin didn't want me back--

I fisted the wet ground, my fingernails digging into soft soil and cool, silken blades of grass.

If I could have grabbed all my blankets from the bedroom and made my bed outside in the yard, I would have. Then I wouldn't have to hear Tarin one wall away and imagine his dark sleeping locks on his white pillow, his breaths coming through the plaster and wood and entering me. His essence lingering in my dreams. Opening me. Destroying me.

# Chapter Ten

*Tarin*

The kid could move fast.

I heard the scamper of his footfalls and, even back here to the side of the house in my office, the slamming open of the French doors, the thump of hard shoes on the wood veranda flooring.

Alli'd gone out back. Like a flash of wind. A breeze.

I felt old and set in my ways and out of date, like someone from a dusty book you haven't picked up since you were a kid.

Like that old clock on the mantle you barely look at anymore but it still ticks.

I wasn't old, but Alli made me feel old. Here I sat at my desk denying my desires, thinking that made me moral and right, trying to teach him. Talking about Omega guardianships. Thinking of him like a step-son who needed to be taught to hunt, then firmly nudged out of the nest to fly even in a world that defied him and put up stop-gaps at every turn.

I was adamant about my Omegas. They could succeed while the world took its time in doing the right thing and granted them the equal rights they should have had all along.

The ancient times were in our Alpha blood. The times when Alphas fought to the death to mate Omegas, to bind them to them, to own them body and mind. Our world still obeyed some of the ancient laws, and Omegas suffered for it.

I wouldn't have it. Not in my home.

It was never my goal to sleep with my Omega guests, my students, my wards. I stood by that as it made me a better Alpha, more pure than the rest of them.

I went to one of my two office windows and drew back the curtain, peering out. Through the paned glass, the view showed me the back of the side yard and, if I craned my neck just right, part of the backyard that wasn't blocked by the veranda itself.

I waved my hand behind me to lower my office light so I could see better.

The shapes in the yard coalesced to familiar bushes, plants, a birdbath, some tiki torches beside three stone benches. And one other object. A boy kneeling. The grass and gardens surrounding him.

In daylight he would be encased in emerald this time of year. Now the shadows overtook him but couldn't quite obscure his clean white shirt, and the bends of his elbows leading to where he had planted his hands, palms down, in the green grassy carpet.

He looked to be part of the gardens themselves. A boy-shaped bush. A sculpture of young, Omega perfection.

And he was, at that. I couldn't deny it. How my pulse thrummed when he was around. How my skin tightened every time he walked into a room where I was present.

I'd been taking my temperature every night now since he came. Convincing myself it was the early onset of the Burn that had me overcome. Or maybe it was my anxiety of the Burn oncoming, and me unable to find Kee for the last six months. Unable to make any other plans for the fevers and arousals other than packing up a bunch of lube and sex toys and renting a hotel by myself for three days.

Alli couldn't know that every time he offered himself to me, my resolve diminished a little more. My own stupid rules about my wards flew right out the window.

Alli was upset and that upset me.

I was fairly certain he didn't believe me when I told him he needed to take time to settle, that if his assignments were too many and too hard, he could take breaks, take his time.

He still seemed to think he'd failed me with every coming day. And then there were Alli's stares, filled with all his hopes. I was used to everything being on my shoulders, including all the responsibilities for my Omegas here at the house. But not that look Alli had, not that hope. Not that restless fever in his eyes. An Omega fever, which of course Omegas didn't get, not like Alpha Burns. Yes, Omegas responded to Alpha Burns with arousal and readiness to mate, and Alli's looks were even hotter. But I wasn't in the Burn.

I had a question I needed to answer fast.

Should I go to Alli right now?

*Ah yes*, said a part of my mind. *Just to make sure he's okay.*

But the righteous part of me, the part that wanted to do the moral and right thing concerning all Omegas—especially those under my care—said I needed to maintain my distance.

That was a bit difficult if I was dreaming of Alli every night. Listening for him moving around his space through the wall between our bedrooms. Questioning constantly: *Am I entering an early Burn?*

Before I realized what I was doing, I let the curtain drop. My feet were bare, padding down the hall and through the kitchen to the open French doors.

For a moment I stood on the threshold, breathing in the fresh, cool air. Silently, I made my way across the wood floor to the stairs.

He remained still, kneeling in the wet grass, and my feet and the hems of my trousers were soaked by the time I came up alongside him.

"I'm not sitting and getting my ass wet," I said softly. "Would you like to move to a bench?"

Startled, Alli looked up at me, his face bathed in dim moonlight. He looked so young. Ethereal. My pulse stepped up.

His computer began to slide into the grass. He sat back and grabbed it.

"You followed me," he said.

"Come on. Get up." My words came out harsher than I'd intended.

The trees beyond shivered and for a second the crickets stopped. The breeze stopped. All was silent.

Alli got to his knees and stood, clutching his computer.

I led us to one of the stone benches.

He sat with his head bowed.

I hoped the others were settled in their rooms by now, not paying attention to anything else but their studies, or in the case of Farrell and Tev, each other.

"When we first met, you wanted to rob me." I made it a statement of fact. For I could feel it off him that night on the street, the desperation of him, his scent of ice and need.

Head hanging, the words came as night whispers almost lost in the late silences. "Until I scented you."

"Really?"

"Yes." Low. Shy. "After that I wouldn't have. I never would have done anything that might hurt you. I just wanted to give myself to you. And maybe you'd pay me so I could get off the street for a few nights."

"What changed your mind?"

"You did."

"How?" I needed him to say it.

"Something. Something else. Something more about you. Not like the others I saw picking up all the corner boys. Nothing like them."

The knowledge of what this was began to dawn on me, but I wouldn't face it. Not yet. Not until I heard more.

"Tell me how you see me."

"I—I can't. I don't know!" His voice shot out stronger.

"You would have sold yourself." It was a question. And not a question.

"It's not a crime." His tone went up.

"But more dangerous when the Alphas aren't vetted."

"I was very hungry."

"Yes, I remember."

Finally, he looked up, and his face had fallen, drawn and sad. "Are you trying to tell me I did wrong? You've slept with a corner boy before."

That stung all the way to the pit of my stomach. I'd tried so hard to help Kee.

I bit down on the inside of my lower lip. I glanced away but not before I saw Alli's mouth open and his eyebrows go up.

"I'm sorry," he whispered. "I shouldn't have said that. I don't know what's wrong with me."

"The world isn't black and white. Neither are people. But we say things and think things sometimes as if the world works that way."

I sighed. I leaned back against the cold stone of the back of the bench. This boy—he was going to be my undoing. It wasn't that I didn't want him in return. But I couldn't face that. Not yet.

And then there was the fact that when I gave him his wings, he'd fly. They all did. Kee flew before I'd even caught him. He'd been wanton and crazy.

But Kee never wanted to be like the others, to study or learn his own way in the world apart from what his body could do for Alphas, and his drugs could do for his mind.

He was lost before I'd found him.

Alli wasn't lost. He was far more dangerous to me because of that.

My heart could not stand being broken. A voice in my head startled me. *Whose can?*

"I'm sorry," Alli repeated. "I had no right to say those things to you. In your office. I'm sorry."

The feeling in my chest was like grinding gristle and bone every time Kee didn't answer his texts or messages. For the last year. Not just these six months he'd been gone.

Yet this boy before me exuded a scent like an elixir my body craved. I had been denying it for four days. Four short days. Not long enough to know him, or understand a thing about this feeling.

And yet, too long, it seemed. For every part of me craved him. And as I had that thought, Alli said in a voice that seemed to brighten the dark just a little.

"I always wondered about fated mates. Is it a real thing? I read it in books. All fiction. But the feelings were so strong, like if—if only it could be a real thing. A call and an answer. Nothing more complicated than that."

"You don't like complication?" I asked. My breaths were getting shallower. I had felt the fated call with Kee. Or so I'd thought. But I didn't believe in that tripe.

"It's how the world works, I know. Life is complicated. Shit, you must think I'm such a shallow kid."

I let out a low laugh. Yeah. I did. But I wasn't going to say it aloud. I only and always had the urge to make him feel better from the moment we met.

"Not always," I said.

"But those books you gave me. The math, the science. It *is* complicated. All that, trying to explain the world around us, when I can plant a seed and just watch it grow. That I understand."

No. Not so shallow after all. Maybe just a starry-eyed boy.

"You need time." I let out a sigh. "Time for everything. You just got started here."

"I'm eighteen." He said it like it was an honored title and claim.

"Yes, and yet it's not like it's some magic number when everything changes and you are suddenly whole, all that you can be. A legal adult and an adult are two different things."

"You're making fun of me."

"No."

"It's a magic number for Alphas, though. They get their first Burns within days or a week of turning eighteen. Just because we don't get the fever doesn't mean it's not a rite of passage for us as well."

I heard his breaths, short and tight.

"You want to talk about rites of passage?" I asked.

He let his computer slide off his thigh and onto the bench beside him. Then he pulled one leg up, hugging his knee. "You mean the Burn?"

"Yes. The Burn. What they teach and how it really is— two different things."

"How?" The curiosity slipped into his question along with the downward slope of his shoulders; he was waiting for me to talk more. For the words I would say.

It was a mistake. It would only make things more intimate between us if I explained. But it was what he needed.

"My first Burn experience. You really want to hear it?"

"Yes! Was it good? Was it everything they say it is for Alphas?"

I let out another half-laugh. Ah, the exuberance of youth.

"Hmm. Let's just say that for me, it was underwhelming."

"Why?"

"The Omega, for example, was extremely experienced."

"A farm Omega?"

I nodded.

"Isn't that good? Isn't that what you like?"

"Well. I really didn't know what to expect. I was almost exactly your age. And a virgin. And he was impatient. Expecting me to be something else—I don't know—a certain way, when in reality I had little clue. All I knew was I was burning up, wanting release. But he didn't smell quite right, and in fact it was bothering me, the scent, not right. Not sweet, but sort of dry and oily at the same time. Acrid. I later found out he wore a perfume I hated. Maybe I was even allergic."

"Oh wow." Alli breathed deeper now, slower.

"I didn't find him enticing at all. I couldn't really remain close enough to him to do any good. In the end, he ordered me on the bed and, well, used his hands and mouth until the Burn was done. He wasn't at all satisfied, and I came away thinking I was the worst failure the world had ever known."

Alli said, softly, "Oh. Gods."

"So there you go. Rite of passage. How does it sound?"

"But it got better, right?"

"Of course. You grow up. You mature. You learn."

"That's why you don't want me, then." He looked up. "You said it before to me. You don't like virgins."

My heart twisted. I closed my eyes. Why did he have to talk like that, in a voice that was so sweet, and deep, and pure? Why did he have to smell like my favorite summer day from childhood, like longing and rain which I loved, and night all wrapped up, tidy with a red bow, as if waiting for me to unwrap?

I had never encountered it so right before. Not like this. The scent, the want, the sweetness. It was too much.

"It isn't you," I finally said. Keeping my voice low. "It's everything. Timing. I wasn't expecting--"

"I know. You were expecting Kee."

Kee who didn't love me. And really, did I even love him? He was impossible to hold. To see clearly. Always out of focus, always running toward me or away without a second's notice or a glance. Taking what he wanted. Laughing to the outskirts of his own addictions and never wanting to come back.

Never really wanting me.

But yes, I had been expecting him.

And now another lived in his room.

"I don't know if I could be better." Alli made the statement as if out of context.

"What?"

"But I will try harder than any of them. I will!"

"Any of whom?" My lovers?

"Your Omegas. Your Burn partners. All of them." He bent his head, his hands weaving on his lap. "I know, I keep saying that. I shouldn't. But I want you to know it. I smell you and I know. I would be better. For you."

The boldness of him. I should have been incensed. Instead, all I could think was: *How brave.*

I smelled him and I knew, too. But I couldn't get past the wall in my head.

This Omega, small and young and a runaway who had never known his own rights, or learned proper math and science, reached out to me then, and put his hot little palm on the top of my forearm, letting it rest there.

With that one touch, everything changed.

# Chapter Eleven

*Alli*

Against my palm, flame.

It burned but didn't hurt.

Being this close to Tarin flipped my heart upside-down and sideways. I wasn't sure what to do, but it was as if I had no control. Over my body. Or my mouth and what it said to him.

*Fated mates.* It wasn't real.

This was just a crush. A stupid child's crush.

The night was so damp the moon fogged up for a moment.

He didn't want me back. He was just being kind, sitting there, not moving, telling me intimacies about his first time. His rite of passage.

Tarin was so much older than I, and smarter. I was boring. I was silly. But I kept thinking I could be good for him. I didn't know any other Alphas, but this was the Alpha my body wanted. I wanted.

Suddenly, his low voice broke the songs of the crickets. "I scented you, too."

"What?"

"Right away. The moment you decided to follow me from the Trenches, past the bars and the strip clubs, past the massage and tattoo parlors and down into the darker streets."

"You sensed me, of course. You practically attacked me." I smiled into the dark at the memory of his hands holding me tight against the closed storefront wall, his body nearly pressing me into the brick and stone.

"I heard you. Yes. But I scented you, too," he repeated.

What did he mean? I waited, but he didn't speak further. He didn't pull away from where my hand pressed his arm, either.

Then I sensed something deeper. An assurance in the back of my mind like a warm flicker with the *feel* of Tarin that my crush was not simple, and not necessarily one-sided.

Subconsciously, I'd known. Which was perhaps why I'd continued to be forward and brave when I thought I was rejected.

In a small voice, I said, as if I knew what I was talking about when truly I didn't. "It's more than the scent."

No response.

"Tell me you feel it. That I'm *not* crazy." My words came out of me as if from someone else.

A warm hand closed over mine against his arm. Holding me there. Fingers pressing the tops of my knuckles, soft but firm.

A pulse from my core, like white noise, blocked out everything for the next few seconds. Electrical surges shot through my chest, stomach, arms and legs.

I held back a groan, but a tiny sound escaped my throat, desperate, pleading.

Finally, an answer. A single utterance.

'Yes."

I wasn't sure at first what the word meant, or who spoke it. When I realized Tarin was answering me, addressing my question straight on, my head went back and I sought his gaze.

Yes, he felt it, too? Yes, I was *not* crazy? Maybe I wasn't his type, but he sensed it, the *more* between us, the pull, the tug, the flip of the heart.

There was some amount of pain, too, in that single syllable.

Tarin had had issues with Omegas. Concerns of the heart. Of trust. I didn't know how I knew, but it was there inside me, the knowing along with the longing along with the irresistible craving for him, like the stars when you're a kid and you first really *see* them. Like long nights when you can hear the rain and it just goes on forever and you know you're a part of it, never ending, and there is no such thing as birth and death, just being. Just pure and inspiring energy.

Tarin leaned into me at that moment when I was remembering, when the essence of the feelings inside me manifested to experience, and artful need.

I felt his lips before they even brushed my forehead, the surge of their plush texture, the muscle of the kiss pressed into my skin. He raised his free hand and put it at the back of my head, threading his fingers through my hair.

The world became a rush of noise and sensation, the dark alive, the moon brighter than the longest day.

And I was precious. For a few moments in his arms, I was rare and new and he wasn't being polite about it, or kind, or indulging my boyish crush. It was real, and he was letting me know it.

I raised my head and his mouth slid over my forehead, down the bridge of my nose to my upper lip. I opened my mouth a little and kissed where I could reach. Above the chin. The underside of his mouth. The pressure encompassed the gesture, and before I knew it his lips fit perfectly against mine.

I wanted to drink him down.

These days when the world yearned for better things, I yearned more to have this feeling. To feel the closeness of this man, this Alpha. I was a selfish brat. Gray had told me this many, many times as he dragged me to the closet, as he paddled me with his many wood and metal devices.

But I couldn't deny that in this moment this was what I'd been living for. What I'd dreamed of my whole young life. Not college degrees or owning businesses, or even an Omega's freedom to be equal with his Alpha counterpart, but this. Always this.

Was it always like this for Omegas? Was I different? Or was what surged between me and Tarin special?

His lips moved gently over my whole mouth, tasting me for many seconds before he finally pulled away.

I gripped his forearm hard. "Don't."

Tarin's breath came out in a whoosh. "That's enough for now."

"For now?"

He looked at me with liquid eyes. "We should not rush into anything. I don't rush."

My fingers clutched him. "Don't you feel it, though? Tell me you do. It's something real. I feel it in my mind."

"Yes."

"We're not rushing, then."

But he'd already alluded to being hurt in the past. I knew his careful mannerisms and his need to help wayward Omegas and his house rules of not sleeping with his wards had been part of the result.

Tarin stood. "Come. It's getting late. And don't you have more studying to do?"

Disappointment reigned.

He held out his hand to me but I pretended I didn't see it. Still feeling the touch of his full lips to mine, I couldn't believe it was over so soon. That he wanted me to go off to my room, away from him, away from this.

I grabbed my computer and jumped up, stalking ahead of him toward the veranda.

I kept my head down as I reached the indoor stairs, listening for him, yearning to know that maybe he followed me. But he did not. I was alone.

I went to my room and plopped on my bed, but I didn't study. I set my computer to the side, lay back against the many pillows, and stared upward in a daze.

My whole body felt charged as if I'd walked through an electrical field. My skin felt cool to the touch, but hot underneath, and my veins thrummed with arousal. My cock pushed hard against my underwear beneath my trousers. In my abdomen, pulses of pleasure trembled through me, keeping me poised in this state, on the brink of excessive need. My asshole felt wet and hot, and I squirmed on the bedspread, trying to get more comfortable but not succeeding.

Finally, I got up, stripping off all my clothes and turning on the shower. First I made the water as hot as possible. When that only annoyed me, I turned it to cool and let it sprinkle over me for a good long time.

I did not jerk off as I usually did when I became aroused. Instead, I let my anger control me—anger that Tarin had seemingly rejected me. That he had just let me go and pushed me to my room to be alone. I knew why, and I knew I shouldn't be angry. He had not told me outright *no*. He had kissed me. Well and thoroughly.

That had not been rejection.

But he put me off, making me feel like an unruly puppy to be swatted away when he went too far. And that was what I didn't like.

After the shower, I walked soaking wet back to the bedroom and flopped on top of my bed again, not caring if I soaked my coverlet. My wet hair immediately dampened my pillow.

I lay in the darkness, stark naked, feeling the air skim across my wet skin, slowly drying it.

My cock stood straight up, leaning toward my belly, heavy and hot. Not time away from Tarin nor the shower made it go down. I didn't want it to go down. I wanted it to remain hard like this, ready and waiting for Tarin. Forever if need be. I didn't want to feel normal ever again.

This buzz, this heady physical excitement stirred my mind round and round.

I hadn't even realized I'd spread my legs, knees up, to expose my hole to the air. It felt open and ready. I was ready. Ready for an Alpha to take me. But not just any Alpha. Tarin. Only Tarin.

Just the thought of his name sent a wave of pleasure through me, making my cock throb.

Tarin said he didn't like virgins, but I knew what I wanted. He wouldn't have to work hard at all to have me. He wouldn't even have to teach me if he didn't want to.

*Tarin. Tarin.*

My mind would not stop reciting his name, sending me to higher realms of ecstasy without release.

I heard water in the pipes in the walls. Footsteps on the hollow floor.

I sat up and lay my head over the headboard and against the wall, turning so my cheek pressed the coolness of the layers of white paint.

I sensed him moving around his room, back and forth. I smelled the fiery cologne of his skin as I imagined him removing his clothing, first his shirt, then his shoes. Next, the trousers. He wore tight black underwear which cupped his heavy balls, and he was erect.

I could see it in my mind's eye and I knew it to be true. All of it. What he was doing. The color of his briefs.

My cock bobbed in the darkness, seeking connection and touch.

I watched him as if I were looking through a window into his room. He brushed his hand across his crotch, lightly cupping his balls before giving a sigh and letting his hand fall. My imagination? No. It had to be real. The image was too well-focused in my mind.

I wanted to be on my knees before him. I craved it like nothing I'd ever craved before. This was a hunger like starvation. As if I didn't eat right now, I'd die.

My mind wrestled with many scenarios. I could lie in bed and stroke myself until I came and then maybe get some sleep. I could do nothing and lie awake all night and let myself suffer in this floating ecstasy. Or I could get up. I could be bold. I could go to him.

The third scenario both excited and terrified me. If Tarin became angry and treated me like a child—which I still was in so many ways despite my age—I don't know if I could handle that. If he tossed me out—of his room or the house—either way, I'd be mortified and left with nothing. So far he'd given me everything, including safety.

Yet, this need inside me crested so high I felt ready to gamble it all to satiate it. I was insane, for sure. Or better, in an altered state. I liked the feeling so much I actually smiled to myself in the darkness, running my hand slowly over my flat stomach and around my cock, never touching it but coming close, so close.

I wanted Tarin's heated body over mine, to be encased in the oven of his Alpha embrace, surging up to be claimed forever and ever. Never stopping.

I heard something drop heavily to the floor next door, and a low curse, though I couldn't make out the word.

Tarin had—dropped something? Fallen?

No, that couldn't be. Tarin was strong and never wavering. The most protective Alpha ever, though I'd met none others. But I knew it. In my heart. He was the epitome of his kind.

Lying in my bed in the darkness, listening to the sounds from Tarin's room made the intense longing worse. My body yearned so hard I thought I might come just from that. No touch. Just overwhelming, fierce need.

He was there in the back of my mind, a caressing thought. He had to feel it, too. How could he ignore me?

Could a person die of desire?

I thought I would break apart.

I got up and threw on my robe, not bothering to belt it in front. Yanking open my bedroom door, I stepped into the dark hall.

Down at the end shone a faint gold light under the window, midway to the floor, as if a nightlight I'd never noticed before had always been there. A beacon to shadows. A way to see the path in the night.

My robe hung open at my sides, revealing everything I was and felt in the moment. My cock pointed straight for

Tarin's door. I walked straight up to it, reaching out and laying my palm flat against the cool, wood surface.

*Please, please let me in.* But I didn't knock.

All was silent within. In my mind I could feel him. He wasn't asleep.

I stayed very still, hand against the door, for a long time. Eyes wide open in the dark. Mind spinning.

He wasn't going to come. On the other side, Tarin was in there ignoring me.

I fell with a soft hush to my knees and placed my forehead against the barrier that kept us apart.

I should go back to my room and try to sleep. I knew it. How could I want someone who didn't want me back?

But he did want me. That kiss. In the dew and the damp and the cricket song. In the late half-moon evening filled with the perfumes of the garden beds and the fresh emerald grass.

He'd claimed me with more than his lips. I wanted to shout it. *You did this! We did it together. You can't deny me!*

Without warning, I fell forward on my hands as the door moved. My head dropped and from my knees I looked up.

Door open, Tarin stood at the threshold in a soft, dark green robe staring down at me. His legs were bare, furred with dark hair that glistened against his skin. I looked up and up, past the shadows at the hem of his robe—no I didn't see a thing—and into his face. Determined blue eyes glared, but the hint of an upturn to his mouth softened the gaze.

"You young ones. Always in a rush," he said.

# Chapter Twelve

*Tarin*

"Get up. Come on."

To find Alli kneeling, practically disrobed, at my door should not have surprised me. Yet, it did. His boldness on the street when he'd followed me was nothing compared to this.

I had sealed the new bond forming between us with that kiss only a few hours ago. And yes, there was a bond forming. I could no longer lie to myself. I could no longer ignore it.

I had thought we would have more time to explore the budding of it. We could sleep on it and be better oriented in the morning to assess and even discuss the potentialities of what was happening between us.

But younger Omegas, especially virgins, had a hard time with the concept of going slow.

Ah, virgins.

"I can come in? Really?" Alli asked.

"Get in. Go sit on the side of the bed."

Alli glanced at the bed, pink rising in his cheeks, and stood, pulling his robe closed as he took a step forward, but not before I saw all. His firm slim thighs, his flat young belly, hipbones and the sides of his ass waiting for exploring fingers to discover them for the first time. His erection was as beautiful as I'd imagined, bobbing beautifully, pink-tipped, arching just before he closed the robe over himself in a quick attempt at decency.

Nothing was decent between us now.

Rushing into things had never been a good experience for me.

His sensations through the tiniest filaments of a new bond still forming had driven me to feelings not unlike the Burn. I admit, half a dozen times this night as I lay in my bed trying for sleep, I'd almost gone to him. My thoughts were outrageous—I had fantasies of smashing open the guest bedroom door, grabbing him from his own bed, throwing him over my shoulder and carrying him back to my room.

But here he was. And I could put that fantasy to rest. Maybe.

In the time after our kiss, I had briefly thought of Kee, how he'd stay in that room next to mine for only intervals of days, nothing more, how I'd wanted more, craved it, but Kee would have none of it beyond my Burns.

He'd laughed at my offers of a ward-ship.

Kee had never come to my bedroom door, leaning against it.

Now Alli was front and center, needing me even more after I'd sent him to his room, and I was familiar with that feeling. I knew how much it hurt.

I'd made the mistake of thinking Alli knew who I was when he'd followed me down the street. That I took Omegas into my home. That I was easy and generous with my money. But he hadn't known any of it. He'd trailed my scent, tracking it in a simple manner. He had not been looking for an education or a guardian even though he needed both.

He'd wanted me from the start. He'd known before I did what our mixed scents meant, what his feelings were even if he couldn't put them into words until we sat on the outside bench tonight.

Fated mates.

Omegas were known to be more intuitive than Alphas. He'd found me first. If he hadn't, as closed off as I was, I am not sure I ever would have noticed him.

"I—I didn't mean to intrude--" His voice started in a whisper and ended on a firmer note.

"You mean intruding on my thoughts?"

He opened his mouth to answer, then closed it, staring up at me with narrowed eyebrows.

"I know it can't be helped with a new bond."

"A—a bond?"

I nodded and his eyes got very wide.

He continued. "The link between us—yeah, I felt that. But I thought bonding came during an Alpha Burn. And—and--"

"Knotting?" I finished for him.

His lips went into a tight line and he blinked fast. He gulped.

"That's true when both partners desire to form a bond," I said. "But there are spontaneous bondings that happen as well. They're more rare. And with fated mates, some myths talk of bonds happening before the two parties ever meet, and they search endlessly for the other until they find them."

Alli had an odd look on his face that communicated both fascination and apprehension at the same time. As if he might be punished for this, a thing he could not control. Obviously, he couldn't deny his body even through his nerves. This was all new to him.

It wasn't his fault.

But suddenly his shoulders twitched, and he clasped his hands in front of him tight. They were shaking.

I felt the tremble in my mind as well.

My heart sped up. I knelt in front of him, wanting to put him at ease.

"Look at me, Alli."

His dark eyes peered from beneath his long lashes.

"We have known each other barely four days. You've been away from the farm, the only home you've ever known, for a week. You can't know everything overnight. You can't know what's out there, and what you might want until you begin to live."

His pink lips parted. "I know what I want."

Inside, my smile lit up my thoughts, my veins. The room grew so hot. But how to be sure? For him? And for my already broken heart? Could I take it again? A young Omega offering himself so easily, saying what he wanted, and then changing his mind?

In fairness, Kee and I had never even begun to form a bond. I'd wanted to. Kee had not. I wouldn't have even attempted it with Kee—not without the Omega's permission. Kee had consented to fucking only. Nothing more. Kee's bond was to money for his addictions. He knew how to seduce me, and that I would give it, and that was the only reason he kept coming back.

"I won't change my mind," Alli whispered, as if reading my thoughts.

"You are so young." I reached out and ran one finger down his smooth cheek.

"That's not fair." He leaned back, as if away from my touch. "You keep saying that."

"Is it not true?"

"Yes." He bowed his head. "And you don't like virgins, I know, but I--" His words stopped as if he'd run out of energy.

I'd hurt him with that off-hand remark when we'd first met. He thought I had rebuffed him. It was his street boy forwardness I'd rebuffed, and the sad reality that to eat he was going to have to sell himself.

"I don't like virgins. Not for my Burns."

"What does that mean?"

"It means when I pay for chattel during my Burns, I want chattel, nothing more. Someone with experience. An Alpha's Burn might seem intimate and thrilling at first, and all about finding love because the Burn is the facilitator of mating, of virility, of perpetuation of the species. But it's quite cyclical and routine. It can mean nothing, really, unless you're with the right person."

106

"So if you want to just get through the Burn, satiate it, you need someone who won't take a lot of your time distracting you."

"Yes."

"I could be that, though."

"My dear, you're already a distraction."

He looked at me with questions in all his features. "But-
-"

"Alli, I'm not rejecting you. I'm not in the Burn."

"Oh." He pouted. He frowned. Then his face relaxed. "Oh!"

Now I allowed a small smile. I suppressed a shudder. This one could cut me deep if he wanted. If he decided things weren't working out.

"You don't hate me, then." He gave me a smug look, one of his cheeks puffing out more than the other.

"I don't know you well enough to hate you."

"You don't know me well enough to love me, either."

"I've never experienced the fated mate syndrome. But I can feel it here." I tapped the side of my head. "Hunger, want, need. Affection."

He nodded slowly, but still looked disappointed.

"It is too soon," I continued. "But here you are. Wanting to try."

"Do you want to try?" he asked. A hush of air followed that last word.

The arousal between us grew more potent.

I had no choice but to be honest now. I couldn't hide or deny it anymore. "Sweetheart, I've wanted to try since I met you."

His mouth opened. Silent. Speechless.

I reached out and placed my palm over his locked hands. The heat from his skin and emanating up from between his legs was like fire. It licked at my wrists.

He was still erect beneath the cloth of the robe. I didn't have to see it. I sensed it. I knew.

My own cock was heavy at my center, rigid and poking at the front of my own thin robe. The sensitive tip rubbed the satin material. Soon there'd be a wet stain. I wanted this young man. This still almost-boy. He made my body feel things beyond cycles and morning masturbation rituals.

I leaned in and put my mouth over his open lips, covered his 'O' of surprise with my own lips, licking my way inside.

His hands unwove from themselves and lifted to my chest. Where he touched me, little infernos began to brew underneath my skin.

There was no going back now.

We were doing this.

He was warm, so warm, and the litheness of his body was astonishing where I touched him, beginning at the shoulders.

I almost feared I would crush him. But I'd learned over the years, Omegas were strong. They bent at their own wills. To force them took a different force, a cruel strength. Though it happened, that could get an Alpha jailed, or worse.

But that sort of crime did not happen to my Omega bed partners. Not on my watch.

The lights in the room seemed blinding. My mind was filled with gold ash, blurring everything but the young man right in front of me.

As I pulled back from the kiss, his brown hair tumbled into his honey-dark eyes. He was bright and shining, light reflecting off his eyes, his mouth, and the curving waves of his locks.

The air hit my mouth, cooling the kiss that lingered there.

He stared at me, eyes wetter than normal, and whispered, "It's okay, then?"

"You decide." If I were the rampaging sort, I'd have bent him over already and plunged my aching self into him. Every part of my body strained for him now, wanted him.

"I decided two days ago. No, three. Hmm." He scrunched up his cheeks and eyebrows. Glanced about left to right. "I'm on your bed." Gasped once as if in shock. *"I'm on your bed!"* He let out a sweet chuckle. "Do you need me to say more?"

"Yes."

"What?"

"Say yes."

His chin went down, then up. His mouth pressed tight, then opened. "Yes."

With that one word, he wound his arms around my neck and pulled me down. Down.

It was easy to follow the tugs, the pressure on my neck, and the way his legs spread to accommodate me. Did his robe spread open as well? I wanted to look down again, see for myself, but our mouths came closer and the draw there was tight and firm, as if this little Omega already had a rope around me and was pulling me in for the final trussing and score.

Omegas always had a way with me. I don't know if it was me or them. Or simply the Alpha/Omega lure. But they had a kind of spell that charmed me until I was all theirs.

But never had I felt a bond begin. Not with any of them. Which told me their part of the relationship had different means to an end than mine. They were into me for lust or money, no bond.

This one, though—he frightened me. He didn't seem to want anything *but* me.

Fated mates. I never believed in it.

Until now.

*Let me, let me*, I thought. *See you. Take you. Want you more.*

I kissed Alli all around his lips, brushing my chin to his, pressing my nose to his cheeks, nuzzling. I felt a bead of liquid drip from my cock and tickle the underside of my tip.

I rarely felt arousal outside the Burn after my twenties. Not even for Kee. At fifty-two, I figured a bonding might only happen now by some miracle. No Omega had ever been the right one, and I figured it had to be something in me. Something off or different I couldn't name.

Now. Alli. Too young to know anything. But knowing more than I, it seemed.

My body covered his. His arms and legs came up and around me and I felt his hardness press against my stomach. So young and stiff and willing.

Alli groaned. I had to remind myself this was a first time for him with another. With me.

But it was a first for me as well, because I couldn't remember wanting another more outside the Burn. Not like this encompassing euphoria that pulled me to him, like a siren call and I was lost upon his shores.

Did he even realize how much he affected me when I let down all my barriers? Even I hadn't.

I lifted him from the shoulders, rising and tugging his body further up into the bed. He went lightly, gracefully, hands clutching at the arms of my robe as if he didn't want to let go of me for one second.

His weight was nothing to me. A silken pouch of feathers. My arms around his waist, I could pull him to me with little effort, scoot him where I wanted him in the bed, position him to where I could now see the way his robe fell away revealing his naked body to me.

I knelt on either side of his thighs, my own robe parted but still belted. Not enough for him to see anything yet. But looking down, I watched his robe slide over his ribs, the skin smooth and pale gold, his flat stomach quivering with his every breath, the cute little round belly button barely a dip in his taut, youthful flesh.

And there, between his legs, jutting from a fine dusting of dark hair, barely a circle around the root, was his sweet cock, stiff and straight, the tip pink as sunset clouds, untouched yet by anyone other than his own hand.

I didn't like virgins. When I was in the Burn.

But this was now, and I was in somewhat of a sane mind. And the freshness of him, the ripeness, waiting to be touched and tasted and taken, waiting to be stroked and caressed and milked and swept away, made my lungs heave.

*I'll be good for you,* Alli had said.

*Ah child, you don't even have to try.*

Alli's gaze was intent on me, watching my eyes as I took in every detail of him. He could feel my arousal through our light link, the bond stirring. He knew. He knew my admiration for him. I couldn't hide it as my mouth watered and I fought for my breath, the heat in my veins a boiling fury.

Maybe he misunderstood the shared feelings between us, for he whispered, "Pretend I'm not."

"What?"

"Not a virgin."

"It's not *all* bad." I let him see my real smile then. Hear my chuckle. "I do like virgins. Sometimes. Such as right now this very moment."

His face flushed and his mouth formed a pretty bow. "Oh," he said. "Oh!"

Pink lips matched perfectly the color of the head of his cock. I leaned over him and kissed him, feeling my robe open more and my cock bob against the satin cloth.

His mouth opened, fresh and wet, like rain, and our tongues met and dueled, making twinges of pleasure sizzle about my balls and lower back, making my cock twitch.

He bent his knees and they came up to press against my ass.

I felt as if I were holding him down, but really this boy had me completely enthralled to his will. Roped and tied. Slung over his heart.

He lifted his hips to me. My knees tightened against his thighs. I ran my hands through his hair and it was like water through my fingers, so light and cool and smooth.

He smelled of summer twilight and there I was running lost through amber and orange skies.

I groaned into his mouth and nearly fell on top of him, only to have him make an answering noise and pull me closer.

The sweetness of him! This was about forgetting the world for a while. Existing only for him. About what I could give him. What he would deign to receive from me. If I could bow before him, I would. Omegas should be revered, but our society somehow had that all backwards.

I rolled to my side, afraid that no matter how hard he clutched me, he might need to breathe.

My robe fell down over me, spreading against my seeping cock.

I lifted myself on one elbow and placed my hand in the center of Alli's hairless chest.

He turned his head, his hand seeking me, landing on the arm that bent over him, my fingers rubbing tiny circles on his pecs, right over where his heart beat.

"I want you," he said.

I kissed him again, then drew back. "Let's take it slow for your first time, okay?"

He gave a heavy sigh. So eager.

"Sweetheart, you need to go slow. Get used to things. You don't need to jump in the deep end your first time."

"I want to."

I wanted to, too.

He pouted.

"No pouting," I ordered, despite the fact he was awfully cute, hair in his eyes and chest heaving. I ran my fingertip over his mouth, tracing the shape of it as it went from pursed to smiling.

"So what does slow mean?" Alli rubbed my arm with his palm.

112

"Ah, we'll see together, okay?"

He lifted up to press himself to me again. I held him, chest to chest, sniffing his hair, kissing his head. His hard cock rubbed against mine with the satin of my robe between us.

He moaned. I cupped his head and kissed up to his forehead, trailing my lips all over him, then pressed him back until I could skirt my lips down his cheek to his jaw, his neck, his chest.

He relaxed then, letting me worship him. My tongue tasted his collarbone, his Adam's apple, then further down to the rise of his breast muscle and the hardening nipple there. I blew on it and he shivered. I licked it several times before sucking the little nub into my mouth.

Alli made a strangled sound and his body arched. I had my head turned so I could see his body spread out. His cock twitched and bobbed up almost straight, pointing at the ceiling.

The look of him—the thought of him so fresh and young wanting me, an older Alpha, thrilled me. And made me want to take everything even slower.

I trailed my fingertips up and down his ribs and stomach as I sucked his other nipple. He groaned and spread his legs, his robe falling entirely away from his body now, encasing only his arms.

For a long while I teased him, which was my pleasure, too, just by watching his body react and by how streams of his desire leaked into my mind.

To think—this little one who had followed me only a few days ago was mine in this way. In thought and heart. In the body's arousal.

I lifted my head from him and sat up, pushing the robe from his shoulders.

He saw what I wanted and sat up, shrugging out of it, lifting his body to pull it away and toss it over the side of the bed.

Now he was fully naked before me. I ran my fingers over his hips, dipping to the curves of his ass, then down over his thighs. When my hands came back up, he spread his legs and I leaned over him, one leg bent to balance myself, and ran both my palms up the insides of his thighs.

He groaned and bent his knees, lifting up, giving me full view of his tight sac and a shadowy peek at the crevice that led to his hole.

I brushed the underside of his buttocks, just below his balls, and the skin there was so soft and plush I wanted to rub my body and my face all over it.

Later, I would explore him fully, but for now, my little virgin needed my full attention on him, needed to know what it felt like to be adored.

I leaned down and kissed him on the divot of his left hip, licking with just the tip of my tongue very briefly. Then I lifted my head and nearly brushing my chin over the tip of his flushed and bobbing cock, kissed the other hip.

"Tarin!"

I held him still at the waist with both hands, my tongue moving along his hip, sliding along the very lowest part of his belly to the ring of hair around the base of his cock.

"Tarin!" He called out a second time.

"Stay still," I said softly. "It will help."

"I—I can't!"

The way I was touching him was too much. I tried to remember my own first time, and many thereafter when I was so young, how sensitive I was, how energized and eager. It couldn't be helped.

His cock strained almost painfully before my eyes, bobbing sideways as if to touch my cheek.

"This will not last," I said. "But you will feel better in a minute."

"I feel good now. Too good," he replied between panting breaths.

His balls were drawn up tight and his cock wet with his own leaking juices. He could probably come in this moment without me ever touching him but I wanted to touch, to savor, to taste.

"I promise you this will be good," I said, patting his thigh.

"Ungh!" He squirmed a bit.

"I want you to come in my mouth."

He groaned aloud as I brought my lips to the tip of his cock and kissed him, feeling the dampness, licking at his unique and wonderful exuberance. He was sweet like candy, so special. Why hadn't I seen this with my whole mind from the very beginning?

Because I was closed down. Because I was searching for another who would never be for me what I really wanted or needed.

My tongue poked from between my lips and began to lave his tip, his tiny hole there, licking at the pre-cum that poured from him.

He jerked in my hands, which were on his hips, now, and I felt the throb begin as he gave out a long, low yell that took his whole breath.

He was coming and I sucked his head into my mouth and sucked hard, feeling the spurts begin, hard and fast, then I took him all the way into my mouth and held him there, sucking and swallowing.

He screamed, his hands reaching for my head, pressing down, his legs trembling, lifting up from the bedcovers.

His first time with a man in that way, and he was coming apart just as I wanted, just as I hoped.

His young cock was insatiable, filling my mouth with his sweetness.

There was no softening as I sucked him dry. His pert cock stayed erect as I continued to suckle him.

He moaned and moaned until I pulled off, taking him into my arms, letting him rest for a minute. His hard penis pushed at my thigh, and he humped it a little as he buried his face in my chest. He had not had enough, which I had expected from him. From the eagerness that bled through to my mind.

I kissed his forehead, brushing his hair back from his face, comforting him in the glory of his pleasure. He wanted more, but wouldn't say it. I could feel it all through my limbs, and his trembling need still coursing through his firm, slim body.

After a while, I turned him on the bed. He went over easily, and I ran my hands down his back and over his buttocks. His ass was so pretty, jutting up slightly and rounded just right. My palms fit against each cheek perfectly, and I massaged him and kissed him there, and on the tailbone.

Several times he tried to climb to his knees.

"Relax," I cajoled.

He obeyed my every suggestion, but really it was he who had me trapped and wrapped in his Omega mystery, his web of seduction. He was breathing. He was willing. He was my fated mate. He was mine. But more, I had devoted myself to him the moment I kissed him in the garden.

Knowing now the bond was rapidly forming, that our sex would cement it even stronger, I'd already committed before I could even think the words for it. The "always and until the end of time" words recited in ancient ceremonies. Pretty words, but I didn't need them now. The Alpha response was automatic to protect, devote, provide, give all. That was my way, at least, and my downfall, too, for when I felt these emotions before a verbal commitment, it never guaranteed the Omega wouldn't change his mind, run off, and never contact me again.

It hurt to know I'd put myself in this position yet again, but I couldn't control it.

I kissed his ass as he lifted it into my face. I ran my tongue over his tailbone and down, encountering the slickness of his internal Omega arousal.

116

I licked there for a while, then lower to his balls, taking them into my mouth, feeling them tighten.

He lifted himself higher with my arms under his thighs, and I nipped at the underside of his cock, the weight of it making it point toward the sheets.

I nudged it backward with my wrist and sucked it into my mouth again, hearing Alli squeal and groan into the pillows at the head of the bed.

I turned onto my back with my head beneath his hips, lowering him down and into my mouth again. One hand worked the base of his cock, milking it into my mouth and he jerked hard and came again, spurting hard.

I used my weight to push him onto his back again, and caressed him softy with my grip until the rush of his orgasm left him depleted, the semen now only dribbles.

He threw his hand over his eyes.

I smiled. I wanted to laugh.

Did he not think it would be this good?

I could make it better and better for him. This I vowed, silently. The essence of the thought must have brushed over his own mind as he said in a small, almost whiny voice, "Hold me."

I drew him to me again, my own arousal sated on his releases for the moment, but my cock hard as a lead pipe between us.

# Chapter Thirteen

*Alli*

Twice.

Tarin had made me come twice in the most luscious way! He'd used his mouth. He'd sucked me and the feel of that, the hot, incredible suction, sent me flying.

I was still restless, my cock over-sensitive but still half hard, wanting to feel him all the time against me, more and more and more.

I breathed Tarin into my lungs, my nose in his chest, his neck, his armpits. Trying to fill myself with his fire. His starry nights. His dark heat.

I felt like an Alpha in the Burn. I couldn't get enough. I wanted him to fuck me, knot me. Everything. I wanted everything. I was wet in my ass, and quite ready. I could feel the tremble deep inside, the hunger, the clenching of my muscles readying for a mating, craving to be fucked.

It was amazing. All these new sensations. And how deeply I needed to be merged with this Alpha. My Alpha. For he was mine and I would fight to keep him with all my strength.

I felt his cock jut against my thigh, big and hard and strong, and realized I had yet to see Tarin naked. I had been so selfish!

As he held me, as I continued to catch my breath, I worked my hands between our bodies and slipped one between the opening in his robe.

Tarin nearly jolted out of my arms when my fingers encountered his stiff heat, circling around the amazing girth, holding him tight but not too tight so I could run my grip from the base to the tip and judge how long he really was.

I grinned into his chest, kissing him as I moved my hand up and down. He was long and thick, no disappointment there. Huge, in fact, and I loved the idea of him stretching me with that cock, then knotting me, making me feel full and wanted and owned. I wanted it. Badly. Even if it hurt at first, I didn't care.

He'd licked me there, over and over, and I thought I would die of the pleasure. I might have had an internal orgasm as well as external if he'd kept it up. But he fixated on my cock, which I loved just as well. Calling me pretty. Calling me sweet.

I wanted him to fill me up with his seed, coming in me for long minutes as his knot worked up his shaft to the head of his cock with one final explosive burst.

How that must feel to Alphas, so grand! But to Omegas—for me—it would be incredible as well, the way he would stimulate my channel and open me up. I had never had an internal orgasm and I wanted to know it before the night was through.

"I want this inside me," I whispered, tugging at him.

He let out a long, contented "ah" sound, then said again the dreaded words I'd already heard once tonight.

"So eager. You want everything at once. But you need to slow down and savor. I promise. You'll get everything."

"I don't want to wait."

"In time," he replied.

I groaned in frustration.

At that, he rolled away from me and before I knew what was happening, he was on his feet at the side of the bed. His robe was open at the chest revealing strong muscles and skin a shade darker than my own. His black hair hung shiny in his eyes.

I reached for him. He couldn't leave me now. Besides, this was *his* bed. What was he doing?

He leaned down and picked me up into his arms effortlessly, cradling me as if I were a baby, my naked body pressed against the satins of his robe and the full heat of his body.

Instinctively, I wrapped my arms around his neck and pressed my face to his shoulder.

He swiftly took me into the shower and set me down, turning on the water, testing the temperature as I stood in the cubicle watching the water flow from the spout above me.

I was still in a euphoric daze.

Then movement drew my gaze. He undid his belt and his dark green robe shimmered as it slid down his body revealing all of himself to me.

My mouth opened. Water splashed against my lips and tongue and I gulped, but not from choking. It was him, Tarin, who caused my response. His impressive body, now on display for me, took my breath.

Muscles rippled, long and lean, his arms flexing, his chest expanding with his deeper breaths. His stomach was hard and rippled, his hips narrow but strong, and his cock jutted out of a shimmering thatch of black curls, long and hard, the balls beneath weighted by their own hugeness.

After everything that had gone on at the farm, and my short time in the Trenches thinking of my bleak and limited future, to have this fall into my lap seemed unbelievable.

In one week, how had I gotten from there to here?

Fated mates.

I could feel Tarin in my mind, but not all the way there yet. And a tremor sometimes accompanied his emotions, something different from pure arousal for a mate.

He still held himself apart from me.

Impatient as I was, I heard his voice telling me earlier: *Go slow. You don't need to jump in the deep end your first time.*

But it was more than that. Tarin was wary with me. The hesitation in him spoke of more than he let on.

In this moment, how could he still be unsure? My desire for him nearly doubled me over. If he didn't feel the same—

120

I couldn't let myself think that. I reached out and touched his wrist, grasping, lifting his hand to mine. I wanted him under the water with me, hands all over me. I wanted to touch him in return.

To my relief, he stepped into the stall, his body towering over me, tall and strong, taking up most of the room. Everything heated up again.

His hip grazed mine. My hand went from his wrist to his chest and I couldn't help myself, I had to press into his pectoral and run my hand over the curved muscle there, and the tight, hard nipple.

He was solid as stone. Like touching warm wet marble.

My cock sprang up again, half-mast. I felt barely used; I was ready to go, as if I hadn't already come twice.

It had been so good, Tarin touching me, sucking me, but it was as if I had yet to be touched still, deeper, stronger. Maybe it was because Tarin had not yet come. Maybe this incomplete feeling came from him holding back.

I glanced at his huge cock again, which might nudge my belly if I took a step forward because he was that much taller than I, at least seven inches.

And with my mind on inches, I noted his cock was way longer than seven.

"Turn," said Tarin.

I faced the water, my back to him, and from somewhere he gathered a palm full of soap and ran his hands all up and down my body, over and over my buttocks which he seemed to love the shape of, as well as how slippery the cheeks were when soaped up.

I longed for his touch, couldn't get enough. His arms wrapped around me, pulling me against him, encasing me in his embrace. I felt his cock nudge my spine, rigid and strong. The power of him overwhelmed me. I wanted to succumb and succumb.

The soap smelled of camphor and comfort. The water pouring over us was like a hundred warm liquid fingers tracing all over my skin.

Tarin held me, then turned me in his arms. Immediately, I ran my hands up and down his hard chest, feeling the light dusting of hair like the finest fur. My blood went even hotter.

I raised my arms around his neck, hugging him, and suddenly his arms tightened about my hips, his hands finding their way to my buttocks, and he lifted me. I wrapped my legs around his waist, feeling his cock nudge my crack.

With me higher up now, our faces were on the same level. I blinked into his eyes and he surged forward and kissed me.

The water sprayed around us, pattering at my back and shoulders.

He moved one arm so his forearm supported my ass, freeing his other hand, and turned off the water.

With me still in his arms, he effortlessly stepped from the shower stall and grabbed an armful of waiting, folded towels from the counter.

He strode into the bedroom, toppled me onto the bed and began to dry me with soft motions up and down my arms and legs, over my chest and belly, blotting sweetly at my cock and balls. He ruffled a towel over my wet hair, then stood back and dried himself.

I watched him bend and bow to dry his legs. He glistened in the amber lighting. He dried his hair in a wild soft of rubbing of the towel.

His large cock was so hard but so heavy it pointed outward instead of straight up like mine did when erect. It was cut, unlike mine, and the huge swollen head glistened a dark pink. It looked so smooth and soft, while swelled at the same time. I wanted to run my hands over it and stroke the shaft. The balls hung large but taut with a bit of dark fur. They would fill my whole palm they were so big.

122

Of course I couldn't stop thinking about him being inside me, moving in and out, stroking my internal pleasure glands. My hole contracted.

I wanted him to take my virginity now. But I was afraid to say anything that might break this wonderful spell, the current between us electric, joining heart, thought and mind. It was electric.

He smiled down at me and came onto the bed on his knees, his body now over mine, a dark heat I needed, craved.

I'd been so hungry when he found me. If possible, I was hungrier now.

"Are you tired?" Tarin asked in a low, gentle voice. "Do you want to sleep?"

Was he crazy? I shook my head hard. *No!*

He lowered his weight at my side, the bed jiggling, and took me into his arms.

"Kiss me more," I begged.

He didn't hold back, his mouth wet against mine, our tongues dancing together. I rubbed my body against his, feeling his cock at my thighs.

He had so much more control than I did. I'd come twice already and he hadn't come once, yet he was calm and seemed happy to be kissing me again and again.

There was still moisture between us from the shower, despite how well he'd dried me, and our skin tugged and stuck a little to each other. I loved it. It made me feel as if I were more and more a part of him.

My cock, ever hard for him, twitched fuller as I rubbed it against his flat stomach.

His arm came around my shoulder and he stroked my damp hair back from my cheek.

"Alli," he said. "I am sorry I made you think I didn't want you. I did. I do. I was wrestling with something else in my head. All right?"

"It's all right," I replied, just glad he'd noticed me. Glad I wasn't doomed to an unrequited crush. Because this was—this was more than a crush. It was everything.

What he was wrestling with, I didn't want to think about. He'd told me he didn't sleep with his wards. But in reality, I knew it was about Kee.

I shut my eyes against the light and that thought.

"I want you in me," I heard myself whisper.

His fingers wove through my hair; he pushed me onto my back until he was half on top of me, kneeling between my legs, and I could feel him looking down at me but I did not open my eyes.

"We'll work up to it," he replied in that resonant tone that sent hot blood straight to my toes, and my cock.

I wanted to cry. Like some spoiled Omega brat. But I wasn't spoiled. I'd lived a farm life, had few possessions I could actually call my own, and a house-dad who luxuriated in punishing and threatening me.

But right now I wanted so very very badly. It made me feel like a spoiled child.

Tarin was fifty-two. He knew what he was doing. I had to trust him.

I sat up, my hands at my hips supporting me, my knees bent around Tarin's thighs and hips. My cock pressed my tummy, straining again. Always at the ready.

I opened my eyes.

Tarin was raised up on his knees between my legs. His hands stroked down my chest.

I saw his cock and again wanted to touch it. He'd already done so much for me.

"Let me." I reached out one hand and placed it on his hip. "Touch you."

He let out a soft laugh.

"You're so beautiful," I said. "You can't deny me this."

His eyebrows came together. "Beautiful? I haven't had someone say that to me in a long, long time."

124

*Not even Kee?*

"Well, you are. It's a fact we simply cannot deny." I grinned up at him.

"And you're beautiful as well."

"Yeah yeah, and too young and a virgin, ick, I know." I smirked at my words.

He let out a quick breath, followed by a sound like a half-moan, an exclamation of surprise.

His hand went to my mouth and traced my lips. I did the same to him, my fingers on his mouth, the tips tracing just inside his mouth, feeling his heated breaths.

"I want to touch you. I want to make you come." I sounded like a petulant boy.

He seemed to like my words, though.

"How will you have me?" he asked.

"On your stomach first. I want to touch you all over."

Immediately, he climbed over my legs, his cock bobbing—how I wanted to feel it, but soon, soon. He lay face down at my side and his magnificent shoulders and back were revealed to me, all muscle and sinew, all ridges of spine and rib and shoulder blade, rippled under smooth, dark honey-toned skin. His waist narrowed on to his slim hips and buttocks, which curved gracefully toward his thighs.

The ass was fleshy, but taut and firm, almost bulbous, and such a turn-on. I rubbed my palms down his back to feel him, his skin as silken as I'd imagined, and heard him groan.

I pushed down harder, giving him a brief massage, and his body seemed to sink lower into the bedclothes.

Good. He was liking this. Relaxing.

I know I moved too quickly, but I couldn't wait. I had to touch those rounded globes. I couldn't resist.

Skimming over his waist and lower back, finally my fingers glided over his cheeks. So soft and smooth, the curves lusciously graceful. Up and down my palms went, over and over them before I dug my fingers in—just a little.

He grunted and his hips rose up about an inch.

I lightly touched the crack, one finger exploring. He didn't say a word about it. He let me spread him, let me look and touch the furred aperture. I did nothing more than that before moving on down to stroke his thighs, inside and out, down the backs of his knees and calves to his ankles, to his toes.

I massaged his feet for a few minutes, knowing how good that could feel because back at the farm I'd had a friend who had a foot fetish and liked to give foot rubs.

When I was done, I said very curtly, "Turn over."

Tarin obeyed. The bed shook. I laughed as the shaking of the mattress almost made me lose my balance.

On his back, flat, he was more beautiful than ever, his dark hair haloing him on the white pillow, his blue eyes hooded, his chest rising and falling with somewhat rapid breaths.

And his cock, prone to gravity, rested straight up on his belly, the tip shiny with pre-cum.

That I could make him feel this gave me a sudden sense of power I'd never felt before, not even when I ran away. I wanted to find myself, feel my own energy, that I wasn't some useless Omega to be punished and threatened with institutionalization. But I had not yet had time to find that, so this feeling was new to me.

I started at his face, cupping his cheeks, his jaw, running my fingers over his lips again. He smiled for me, showing white teeth.

I caressed his shoulders and chest, and ran my fingertips over his nipples, which made his stomach flex and his cock jerk.

I kept that up for a while until he tossed his head a little and shuffled his hips to one side as if impatient.

I ignored his cock and went on to his stomach, tracing the muscles, and the dents in his hips, then down to his thighs, his calves, his feet.

When my hands traveled back upward to his center, delving between his legs, I encountered his balls.

My cock throbbed in empathy as I touched them, cupped them in my palm, felt their weight.

Tarin moaned. There was a little dribble of liquid on his belly from his cock.

I played with his balls but was too tempted by that amazing cock to prolong Tarin's torture.

I ran my palm up from the root of his shaft to the tip, up and down. I had never touched another man's cock before Tarin. He was my first in everything other than kissing—I'd kissed a boy before, but not in the way I'd kissed Tarin, not in the way Tarin kissed me back.

His huge erection was firm and hot to the touch, alive with blood and need and want.

I glanced up at his face. Tarin's eyes were wide open, staring at the ceiling, his bottom lip caught between his teeth.

I ran my hand up and down, looking back at my treasure. I'd learned the knot for Alphas came from the root of the cock first, and from there like a round nodule swelling the shaft, moving up slowly toward the head as the semen spurted out, as they orgasmed to fill an Omega in a full mating designed not only to give them pleasure, but to make a baby.

I circled the root of Tarin's cock with my thumb and forefinger, pressing in, and he moaned in pleasure, tossing his head once. Otherwise, he didn't move, giving me free reign to explore as I pleased.

I brought his cock straight up so it pointed toward the ceiling, and so I could see its glistening, cut tip naked and full before my eyes. So different from my uncut cock, so gorgeous.

Slowly, I ran my grip up his shaft, milking him. The tip swelled a bit as I made that motion, and the tiny hole in the little crevice at the head beaded with more liquid.

Without giving it much thought, I leaned down and licked at that bead of moisture, the slight salt-bitter on my tongue making my heart pound harder, and the blood rush in my ears.

Tarin made a loud sound, almost a yell.

So I did it again. And again as I milked up and down his huge shaft, licking the tip with my tongue all over and around the head, wiggling around his hole, lapping faster and faster.

Tarin made more noises, and his head went back on the pillow exposing his neck.

I put my free palm flat on his belly, and kept milking and licking until he lifted his hips and gave out a strangled cry.

Hot streams of liquid hit my face and lips and the pulse of the cock in my grip contracted over and over as I licked the head. It kept spurting and I put it in my mouth then, sucking at it.

Tarin cried out and more hard spurts filled my mouth.

Over and over he came, filling me up until I had to swallow.

It was fantastic, the taste of him, the pleasure of him, knowing I was making him crazed and euphoric, knowing I could take him to that extreme point and he trusted me enough to let me do it at my own pace, never demanding, never even speaking throughout the entire scene.

I held him firm in my grip, and could feel when his contractions finally slowed, when the orgasm receded.

I licked away at the shining head a little more before coming up over his chest, lying down on top of him, and putting my chin to his.

Our eyes met.

"Well?" I said.

His breaths feathered against my nose and cheeks. He was still overwhelmed.

"You need practice." His voice sounded strained.

"What?"

"Yes. More. You need to do more of that. You can keep practicing on me any time you want."

I laughed aloud, then kissed him hard on the lips. "You're so mean!"

He grinned against me, then said, turning to catch his breath, "That's the only way you young ones can ever learn."

# Chapter Fourteen

*Tarin*

Alli curled against my side, his sweet head on my chest, his breath blowing soft and hot against my nipple.

Just holding him while we slept. That was all it took. I was hard again.

The morning light flowed beige and pink through the curtains. I glanced at the clock and saw it was late. Did I care? No.

The boys could take care of themselves downstairs. In fact, breakfast was probably already over. They were self-starters. They were all probably studying.

I didn't spend every breakfast with them anyway. But I'm sure they did wonder where Alli was.

I kissed the hair on the top of his head, which was soft against my jaw, my lips.

He squirmed against me but did not wake.

I lay in the silence of my room with my mate in my arms—for that was what he was, there was no denying the mental link between us fueling the rush of a newly forming bond—and let myself float on the waves of tenderness and arousal he brought out in me.

For Alli, it would be urgent, but for me I loved feeling aroused and full and good with no Burn, no rush to end things. No need to control the Omega in my arms to bend to my pleasure.

After awhile, Alli woke, his long lashes trembling as he hugged me tight and opened his eyes.

I stared down at him as he raised his head from my chest. His cock was hard against my hip and he moved to release it but it rubbed up and down and before he could stop himself, or possibly knew what he was doing, Alli was humping my side.

"Well, then, you're awake in more ways than one," I said.

He bit his lower lip, then scrambled up on one elbow, leaning over me to give me a kiss. His hand came up and touched my hard cock which was lying stiff against my stomach once again.

"So are you," he replied.

Our lips met.

After that kiss, it was all over for about the next twenty minutes. It didn't take me long to lick him to full hardness and suck out his first orgasm of the day.

Alli made a repeat performance of last night, licking me and stroking me until I couldn't stand it. It was so wonderful I couldn't stop coming for quite some time.

"Wow," he exclaimed.

All Alphas were potent, but some more than others. I was one of those who expelled a lot of semen. It was hereditary.

When we finally got up, showered and dressed, the light from the day was intruding in bright shafts along the hallway and from the big windows facing the kitchen.

The other boys were not around, which was good. I didn't want to feel like I had to explain anything yet.

I made Alli sit while I fixed us a nice brunch of omelets and bacon and fried potatoes. I liked taking care of Omegas, but my mate brought that out in me even more. I wanted to provide for him. Everything. And that meant it was a true pleasure to cook for him.

"Do you have to go to work today?" Alli asked, crunching on his bacon.

"No."

He grinned. "Is it because of me?"

I gave him a side-long look. "No."

He pretended to pout.

Later, I had Alli take me into the yard and show me what he had in mind for a garden.

I showed him an entire plot he could have all to himself.

He looked dazed and excited at the same time, the light hitting his eyes and making them glow amber.

"I want cucumbers and squash—it's so pretty—and peas. And maybe a decorative border of lavender and daffodils. It would be really pretty. Oh! And tomatoes. I want those, too."

"And you shall have them," I replied.

For Alli to go from a runaway to this was exciting for me to observe.

Tree shadows dappled the grass all around us. The day was amazing, the sky bluer than I'd ever remembered seeing it.

Together, we mapped out a border along the grass where Alli would have his own bed for growing whatever he wanted.

He looked up at me through squinted eyes, the light on his face brilliant.

"But I'm missing my studies."

"These are your studies for today," I said.

He hugged me hard, and the world seemed to shift beneath us, though really it was just him, holding me tight, pressing all his weight and his thoughts into me.

He surrounded me with his light, and a craving, a hunger, a lust. And also, the tender beginnings of love. It was the most serene contentment, like a finished fine meal capped with chocolate and wine, only ten times stronger.

We still had the final consummation to perform. Intercourse and knotting. It would fully satisfy the bond and possibly complete it. I hadn't decided if I wanted to wait until my Burn, or do it sooner.

Like tonight.

My new mate was just that irresistible.

The irony was, when I'd been searching for Kee, who I thought I'd loved, I'd found my true love out in the forlorn and rancid world of the Trenches.

Fated mates. I thought it was a myth. But everything had happened so fast, and that was what fated mates meant. It astonished me and made me ecstatic at the same time.

I suppose I could no longer disbelieve the myth.

I looked up and over Alli's head to see Oren coming through the French doors, stepping out to greet us.

We both turned at the same time. Alli went to pull away, but I kept my hand over his shoulders, gripping him harder to let him know it was all right.

"Hey!" Oren shaded his eyes with one hand. "Hi."

"Hi," Alli said.

I nodded in greeting.

"So. I see it's you two. That's great. Congrats." He didn't make a big drama. He didn't appear jealous or shy about it at all.

"Thanks," Alli said, glancing quickly up at me.

"Yes," I replied.

"So are you getting your own garden?" Oren asked Alli.

The slight tension was broken just like that. Alli jumped forward. "Yes! I am! Right here! See? And I'm going to have tomatoes and cucumbers, and well, just everything!"

"Wonderful. They will be the best, too, and I hope you'll share."

"Oh, I will!" Alli sat back on his haunches beside the area we'd staked for the garden bed.

I crossed my arms and watched the two Omegas interact. They were beautiful. All my wards were, but none had affected me so deeply, with an actual automatic bonding link occurring, until Alli. Not even Kee.

And it had happened so quickly.

My entire body craved him now. All I could think of when I looked at him was that I wanted to touch him all over without the barrier of clothes. I wanted to see him naked all the time.

It wasn't like me at all, but I couldn't help it. Already in my fifties and I'd never experienced a bond before.

Fate would say I'd been waiting for my mate. He simply hadn't been born yet when I was an adult. In fact, he had not yet come of age until four days ago, the day after we'd met.

Such a baby.

After a while, we all walked back into the house.

In the afternoon, with the windows open and the breezes filling up all the rooms, we talked away the hours.

Oren, polite as ever, left us alone after a while. Tev and Farrell were never much for socializing other than on movie nights, so they kept to themselves.

I loved listening to Alli talk. He had a low sweet voice, a sound that seemed to enter my body, my veins, my mind, and plummet me into a solace I had craved my whole life but wasn't sure what to call it.

I felt whole with him at my side. This almost-child, this newly blooming man had a piece of me inside him all along, or at least some compatible essence my mind recognized now as everything I yearned for.

We sat on the living room couch, me at the end, Alli on his back with his head in my lap. I couldn't keep my hands from his hair. I wanted to hold his lithe body against mine again, skin to skin.

My body remained hot all day.

I leaned down to kiss his forehead.

He took in a sharp breath.

"Take me upstairs," he begged.

I lifted him in my arms. He weighed nothing to me. Would he let me carry him all the way up to my room?

"We're going to have to move your things into my room," I said as he wrapped his arms around my neck and his legs about my waist.

134

"Yes, please," he replied. "But not now."

*No, not now.*

Up the stairs we went, and he never asked me to put him down.

I drew the curtains but the light still invaded my room. I loved it because I wanted to see him, Alli without barriers, Alli naked for me and wanting me.

He did not beg me, this time, to knot him, but in the mind-link and the bond forming between us, I felt his need, his desire.

Soon, I thought. Soon.

We pleased each other in simpler ways for now, mouth and hands. Kisses and licks.

Afterward, we napped wrapped up in each other, and it was the most peaceful sleep I'd had in weeks.

We woke at the same time.

I sat up, eyeing him up and down, wanting him all the time, but a person had to eat.

"Get dressed," I said.

"What?"

"I'm taking you out to eat."

He brushed the hair from his eyes and sheepishly grinned. "The best burgers again?"

"Better."

I took him to a nice steak house.

When he got the menu, this time he didn't behave as naïve as he had had when we first met. He scanned it instead of reading it from the top. His eyes widened when he saw the prices.

"Don't worry about that," I said. "Order anything you want."

He devoured his steak when it came. This time I knew he wouldn't be sick, though. In a few days he'd gotten his strength back as well as a regular appetite that wouldn't make him sick.

We talked for two hours over our food and our wine. Truthfully, we had very little in common, and yet it was as if we'd known each other for years. He seemed interested in anything I said, listening intently as I'm sure I spoke of things he knew nothing about.

When he told me of his experiences at the farm, I was riveted. Any memory he had, I felt myself leaning toward him, wanting to hear more just because it was Alli.

I wanted to know everything about him. How he became shaped into the young man before me. What had hurt him and what had pleased him. It infuriated me to know he'd been mistreated. I wanted to write to Zilly's immediately with a letter of complaint, but Alli put out a hand to touch my wrist and said, "No."

"Why not?"

"If they know it's me, they could sue you to take me back. Or make you pay for me. I wouldn't want that."

"We're in the middle of a bonding. A bond supersedes all that."

He vehemently shook his head.

"I could make it anonymous. Just a heads up to the warden there."

He lowered his eyes. "I agree the man should be fired, removed so he can't harm another. What I saw him do to my classmate shouldn't happen to another."

"What he did to you shouldn't happen to another."

Alli bit his lower lip.

"So it's settled," I said. "I'll start with an anonymous email."

He nodded. "My word held no weight, but coming from an Alpha, maybe they'll pay attention."

"Oh, they'll pay attention all right."

On the drive home, Alli asked, "When will our bond be complete?"

"Are you asking when will I decide to fully consummate it?"

"Yes." His voice came out strong. He bravely faced me.

"My Burn is scheduled for the fifth."

"Uh." The single utterance held the deepest of disappointments. "That's five days from now."

"It is. But we can have fun in the meantime."

"Does consummation for a bond always have to happen during a Burn?"

"No. But it's the best way. From everything I know, it makes the bond stronger."

"But maybe we can practice."

I laughed. "You are insatiable."

"Tarin, I want you."

"I want you, too."

*

I pulled into my driveway with one hand on the steering wheel and the other held tight by Alli against his thigh.

It was past nine but the lights were all still on in the living room. I figured Oren and Tev and Farrell were having a movie night. They had their own allowances. They could have ordered pizza or anything they wanted.

I drove into the big garage, the door closing behind me, and Alli and I got out. Alli ran up to the entrance from the garage to the house and opened the door, hopping happily up the single step.

I followed, not really paying attention, only to see him stopped dead in his tracks at the wide entry between the kitchen and living room.

The TV was not on, but my three wards sat on the couch, turned all the way facing Alli. Then their gazes met mine.

My heart seemed to freeze for a moment, my skin prickling.

In the EZ-chair, smiling up at me, his raven locks threaded with gold surrounding his head like a halo—though angel he was not—sat Kee.

# Chapter Fifteen

*Alli*

The Omega could stagger a rock with his beauty. He rippled with the ease of it. As if he knew it was his gift, a weapon he could wield like a master.

His curls weren't tight, but loose and full, and they glowed the color of obsidian mixed with strings of gold. Like flame licking shadow. His face was fine featured but strong, not soft, the lines angular and perfect like an impossibly strange and gorgeous cover model people could not stop looking at.

He was taller than any of the Omegas in the room. I could tell by his long legs, how primly they were crossed but both feet still touching the floor.

Broad shouldered, the rest of him looked lean but healthy. His skin had a glow to it, refined, inherited.

"Kee?" Tarin spoke under his breath, his voice catching.

I turned to look at him. His eyes were big, his mouth open. It was as if I'd suddenly become invisible.

This was the street boy Tarin had been looking for?

He didn't look like an addict. He didn't even look like a whore. He had the appearance of a well-kept man who could navigate the world with grace and get anything and everything he asked for.

"Hey, Tarin," said Kee.

"Gods," Tarin breathed. He strode forward.

I stood to the side, watching as Tarin brushed past me and headed straight for the stranger, his former lover.

A fierce ache began in my chest.

Kee. He'd come back. He was who Tarin had wanted all along, the one Tarin sought for all of his Burns. The Omega Tarin had desperately wanted to tame.

Kee stood as Tarin approached. The two fell into an embrace that nearly made me gasp.

Oren glanced my way, but when our eyes met, he couldn't hold my gaze and looked away. The others watched Tarin. None of them were smiling.

Tarin kept mumbling, "Where have you been? Where have you been?"

"I have a lot to tell you," Kee replied, hugging him tight and smacking him on the back.

Tarin said, "I kept texting you."

"I lost my phone."

"You could have found a way to message me. It's been almost six months!"

"I wasn't near phones for a while. I can explain, but—" He turned to look at the others, then at me, eyebrows narrowing.

"But?" Tarin asked.

"But not here. Can we talk in private?"

"Of course."

As I heard those words, my entire body seemed to plummet.

Tarin's body language showed both tension and an eager alertness. Through our link I felt a swirl of emotion I could barely define. Turmoil, yes, but also passion and caring.

I wasn't sure what to think or feel in return. I held all my responses at bay, my self backing off and going distant the way I had when Gray punished me. It was how I coped. It was how I found any strength to keep going, and to finally run.

I made myself take deep breaths. Think nothing. Be nothing. Empty my mind. Hope became black space. My failure milled like shadows at the edges of the walls. My self-worth floated around my head in the shapes of big fat zeroes.

We'd just had a wonderful dinner, such a fantastic day. Tarin had made love to me last night and this morning and this afternoon like I was made of diamonds and light and everything he might desire. And tonight, I had hoped, my virginity might be breached. If I could convince Tarin to do it outside the Burn.

I marveled at how easily the structure of my so-new reality could quite easily fall. The house stood firm; the living room looked serene and the Tarin's other wards sat like the proper students they were, having greeted Kee back into the fold, offering him a chair, offering him company while he awaited Tarin's return, but all I saw was ash and ruin. None of it was real.

I wondered if Tarin would give Kee his old room back. Would I remain in Tarin's room? And how would that be? With Kee around, what would I be for Tarin?

Now Tarin turned to face the room and his wards. And me.

Immediately, Oren, Tev and Farrell rose with excuses that they had things to do, and left to go to their own rooms or the game room.

I turned to go, but where? My room or Tarin's? For certainly, my room would become Kee's again, wouldn't it?

I bowed my head once to Tarin and turned away so he wouldn't see my burning eyes. I couldn't let him know how much I was crying inside, and he couldn't feel it with the link between us flooding us with such confused and muddy thoughts and feelings.

This was Kee. Tarin had cared so much for this Omega. I knew this, and one night between me and Tarin did not give me any right to stand between them. We had not consummated our bond, nor the actual relationship.

I felt I had no power in this moment, nowhere to turn. No place to call my own.

I headed up the stairs, my feet stepping quickly though I didn't really feel them—or anything—and when I got to the long hallway, I stood very still. I was listening for sounds from the living room. Any voice or echo.

But I was also undecided. Which room should I go into? My computer and some of my clothes were in Tarin's room. My other things were in the guest room. Kee's room.

Any move I might make seemed the wrong one.

The house walls closed in. The shadows of the evening from the far window intruded in alien shapes. My vision blurred.

I finally decided the path of least resistance led to Kee's room. I was officially staying there. The permission for that had not been withdrawn.

I opened the door and stepped inside. I'd left a bedside lamp on. It must have been burning since yesterday. The light looked rusty, dingy, aged.

My shoes met the rug and it was all wrong, an unwelcoming surface meant to trip me up. I actually stumbled a little, blinking back my tears.

Every piece of furniture in the room took on a hard-edged countenance. The bed with all its pillows and shiny blue spread looked all too cold now, not cozy and comforting.

I wasn't sure what to do. I turned around and around in the room, trying to think. Should I pack my things just in case? Should I just sit and wait for Tarin to come to me?

I thought about going out back to the garden beds and the stone benches. But I'd have to cross the foyer at the bottom of the staircase and that looked straight into the living room. I would see them. They would see me. It would feel so intrusive.

After some time—I couldn't tell if it was a few minutes or more since my inner clock seemed stopped—I went to the side of the bed and sat, my legs stiff and bent, my back straight.

I inhaled so hard my body jerked the bed itself. Had I stopped breathing?

The link between me and Tarin, so open at dinner, had become muted and strange. Like the beginnings of a storm, clouds on the horizon, light darkening, but you could not yet feel a thing. Every breath I took felt like a pained effort. My body became heavy. All my senses were muted.

I stared straight ahead. Slowly, my eyelids slid down until they were shut and a deep lightless void enveloped me. I was dizzy for a moment, so I lay back, my feet still dangling over the side of the bed.

I heard distant voices. A door banged. Voices outside.

I knew them. Low and intimate, voices intermingling. Kee. Tarin. I could see them walking away. Down the drive and into the dark. Dark heads bent each to the other. Conversation obsessing them, enfolding them until the night absorbed them and nothing was left, not a speck or reflection of hair, clothing, aura.

Gone. They were gone.

At least, this was what I convinced myself of.

I'd read a few required-reading chapters on bonds in my Omega etiquette class at Zilly's. The youngest bonds, newly forming and not yet consummated were the easiest to break.

I remembered the information said there were several ways to accomplish a fairly pain-free break. The Alpha and Omega should distance themselves, the more mileage the better, and the bond would retreat over a period of a few weeks, or even days. Or they could choose to bond and consummate that bond with another partner immediately, and the original bond would disintegrate. Accidental, new bonds that formed without consent could easily be tempered to nothing if no emotional connection was maintained.

With Kee returning to Tarin's life, what I'd experienced last night for my first time could be negated, the link between us easily severed if Tarin decided to choose another. It had been so open between us at dinner and on the way home. I'd never felt so close to another.

A soft whimper escaped my lips.

My feelings of low self-worth came bubbling up—the same ones accompanied by dire threats from Gray that made me run in the first place.

*No!* I wouldn't let that happen. I had everything going for me now. Even if Tarin did not bond with me, I had opportunity. It would hurt, yes, to live here and see Tarin with another, but I would force myself to get over it.

Yet my instinct was to leave. The powerful edge of it tempted me.

I rolled onto my side, drawing my legs up, and pounded the bed with my fist. Tears leaked from the corners of my eyes.

There had been so many things I'd done this past week that had been new, forcing me to be brave. I'd run away. I'd offered myself to an Alpha for money. I'd said yes to higher education, all while practically throwing myself at Tarin.

I could be brave now. Again. I had to.

With a trembling mind I probed delicately at our bond.

A sudden stinging sensation caused me to recoil. What was happening? Was Tarin already closing himself off from me? So soon?

Kee was beautiful, young and strong, with a pride about him that few Omegas possessed. It was easy to see at one glance how Tarin had been pulled into his orbit, attracted and aroused, yearning for knotting and a bond.

Curling myself into a ball, I grabbed a pillow and pulled it over my head. But the stormy pain of that sting and my own growing conviction that I could not offer anything close to what Kee could offer to Tarin tore through me. I wasn't as gorgeous, I wasn't smart, and I wasn't experienced in sexual matters. Certainly, I was not exciting like Kee, who had exuded a charisma that seemed to bounce off the walls of the living room.

I squeezed my eyes tighter as I felt more tears gather. I didn't want to feel this. As I had done when I'd been in Gray's

144

control at the Farm, I started to imagine a brick wall, building it up one piece at a time. Careful, controlled, methodical.

But as usual, it failed to comfort, or make me feel safe.

# Chapter Sixteen

*Tarin*

It could not be true. Kee could not be here. Not now.

And yet the room was filled with him. His scent, his aura, his allure. His shining, raven hair striped with gold, a new hairstyle for him, and utterly becoming.

A windy night. A concoction of wild roaming and never ending thrills. That was what Kee offered.

"Good to see you, Tarin," came the low, enticing voice.

Kee could monopolize a room just by walking into it. The power of him made me crave him. I'd never met an Omega like him.

"Kee. Gods. Where have you been?"

I heard rapid footfalls on the staircase.

Alli had left.

Immediately, I wanted to go to him, but the man in front of me needed to be dealt with. I did not want his brand of excitement anymore. I didn't care about the beautiful sexual positions he'd offered up to me in the past, driving me crazy. It had been six months, but after the last twenty-four hours it felt like years since we'd been together. Decades.

I wanted only Alli now. With all my being.

Kee had denied a bond. I looked at him and felt no desire. I had what I wanted and needed now. An Omega who wanted me. An Omega who craved the bond as much as I, who worshipped me.

I owed Kee an explanation. If he had come back to stay, I had to let him down, tell him he wasn't welcome any longer. I didn't want to hurt him. I never wanted to hurt any Omega. But the circumstances between us had drastically changed.

Before I could utter one word, Kee said, "I came to tell you I won't be back."

"What?" His words threw me. Kee wanted something. He always wanted something.

"I'm here for a quick visit, that is all," he said.

"Uh."

"Tarin, will you sit for a minute? Please?"

He never asked for actions from me using polite mannerisms. A bit stunned, I backed up until I felt the edge of the couch and sat. Hard.

He leaned forward. His dark hair gleamed. He'd cut it since last I saw him, and it was professionally styled with the new gold strands throughout. When he walked the streets he liked it wild and rumpled, like his personality. This was different. This was not the Kee I knew.

Something feathered against the back of my mind, insistent, but I was so curious about Kee I ignored it.

He folded his hands between his knees and leaned forward. "I'm sorry I didn't call you. If you left messages, I didn't get them." He shook his head. "I'm sorry for that."

"You were never sorry about worrying me in the past."

He glanced down at his hands, his breath coming out fast. "I'm sorry about that, too."

Something had happened to this man, this Omega.

"I wasn't near a phone for a very long time," he said. He took a deep breath, then looked up at me, eyes swimming with an emotion I'd never seen in him before. Vulnerability. Yes, that was it. Kee never let anyone see him that way.

"I don't want to go into a long-ass story about all the things that happened to me in the last months, but a lot of bad happened. Then a lot of good."

"I don't—"

He held up his hand. "I was with someone who was not very nice for a while. Thus, no phone. I'm okay, so don't ask me too many questions. I'm barely able to talk about it."

"Kee, did someone hurt you?"

"Yes, but then someone healed me, so don't give it a passing thought."

"That's not possible! I care about you. Of course I gave you a passing thought. More than that! I was so worried. I still am. Are you all right?"

"I'm good now. I promise." He gave me a strange smile. "I needed you to know this. I'm alive. I'm sorry I didn't contact you sooner. You're a good man, Tarin. You didn't deserve to not know. I know you loved me. Maybe you still do. I played on that. So here I am to tell you things are different now."

"Things are different for me, too," I said.

"Really?"

I nodded. "If you can believe it, I met my fated mate."

"Tarin! I'm so happy for you! But—but--" He frowned. "You don't believe in fated mates."

I let out a mirthless laugh.

"Well, then we both have something to celebrate," Kee said. "Because I, too, am bonded now."

"What?"

I couldn't take it in all at once. The Kee I knew seemed allergic to bonding. He would not be tamed. He strutted the Trenches as if he owned them. His drive for sex was as wild as the wind in a winter valley. Cold and insatiable. Searching for something it could never find.

"I was worried about telling you." Kee leaned forward with his hand out, as if to touch me. But he only waved it in the air. "When I finally got a phone again, I kept wanting to call or text, but I—I couldn't."

I thought about the past months, about how I would have reacted. I wanted to think I'd have been happy for him, finally finding *the one* and settling down. But I don't know if I could have been that self-sacrificing and generous.

For a long time I wanted him back and in my life.

"It would have been nice to know you were alive," I said.

"I'm an ass. A total fuck-up. But I met somebody and he—well, let's just say he sort of set me straight."

"What does that mean?"

"It's a long story, Tarin. I'll just say my Alpha is the right match for me."

I blinked hard. I still had residual feelings, but Alli was the one for me now. "Me, too."

Kee's beautiful eyes brightened. "I'm so happy for you!"

"Do you love him? Your Alpha?" I asked.

"His name is Sebastian. Bastian or Bast is what he goes by. And yes, I love him. Our bond is strong. I never knew it could be like this. I never knew I'd survive past age twenty-five, let alone find a bond mate."

Seeing Kee, hearing him talk about finding love, helped me put all the loose and unkempt pieces of my life from the past few years into place. No longer did I have to wonder about Kee. And worry. Now Alli could fit wholly into my mind without any question. My heart could be new again.

Kee had made such an amazing transformation. He still had a bit of that untamed look about him. I was sure he was trouble now and again for the man who called him bond mate. But Kee wouldn't be Kee without his penchant for drama, and his naughty boy tendencies.

I knew I wouldn't miss that, though. As I thought of Alli and our newly forming bond, he was the one I wanted. The one I needed. Even now, my body craved him. I wanted to go upstairs and have my way with him.

The thought sent waves of heat throughout my body. My pulse thrummed in my wrists and neck and chest. He was waiting for me, and a sense of urgency swayed me. The edges of my vision blurred.

"Well, I'm so glad you came home when you did," Kee said. "I'd only just arrived five minutes before your car pulled into the garage."

"I'm glad I didn't miss you," I said.

"I should get going, though."

"Keep in touch?" I asked.

Kee bit his lower lip. So pretty, but not like Alli. No one was like Alli, all the more proof fated mates were real.

"I don't know if it's a good idea," Kee said.

"Of course you're right. What was I thinking?" His Alpha might hate seeing any of Kee's past lovers. And I wasn't sure I wanted to meet this Bastian, either.

"It's for the best." Kee let out a long breath. "You're a good man, Tarin, and I'm glad I knew you."

"I'll admit I thought the worst about what might've happened to you, but I'm so happy to see you healthy. And having found someone."

We both stood at the same time. As if we might be reading each other's minds. But that had never happened between us. We weren't matched in that way.

We approached the front door together and I opened it for him, ushering him through the threshold. For a moment, I felt dizzy. I shook my head and my mind quickly cleared.

I walked Kee to his car parked at the curb, a nice sporty vehicle. His Alpha must be well off, I thought.

Sniffing the air, I detected citrus and sage, and damp grass under the rose bushes that lined my front walkway. I sensed nothing off Kee, more proof that the growing bond between me and Alli was true and right, for a bonded pair scented only each other after they came together.

Shadows loomed as trees rustled in an overhead night wind.

It seemed strangely fitting for our awkward goodbye.

When I reached my arms around Kee to hug him, I felt a sudden sting. A heat washed over me, but not arousal for Kee. It was as if touching Kee had caused me pain and I stopped before I barely brushed him with my forearms.

"Yes," said Kee. "I've found touch to be painful since I bonded with Bast."

"I haven't consummated with Alli yet. Not entirely," I added.

Kee backed up, looking at me with worried eyes. "But you felt it. Like a little shock."

For me it was a bee sting sensation, but I nodded.

"Are you hot? You're perspiring a bit," Kee said.

"I'm fine. Just a little overwhelmed. Still full from dinner. I over-ate."

But that wasn't entirely true.

I shook it off as stress. Yet something else began to brew in the pit of my belly.

"You're not in the Burn, are you?"

"Not for about another five days," I replied.

"It's the bond, then," Kee said softly. He reached out to touch me, then thought better of it and left his hand floating about an inch away from my shoulder.

"Yours or mine?" I asked with a shaky smile.

"Both. It reacts if it sees a threat."

"I'm no threat to you," I said.

"No. My bond is complete. But yours is not. I'm a threat to you."

But that wasn't true. Not anymore. It took seeing Kee again to make it clear to me that I didn't want him anymore.

How quickly things changed. But I had Alli now, and I wanted nothing else. No one else.

Another swell of what felt like a hot wind swirled over me, prickling at my skin. I heard Alli's voice, or something like it, in my mind. Low and even. A murmur I could not make out.

I needed to go to him. I wanted to go to him.

"Hey," Kee said. His eyebrows tented in a V above his eyes.

"I should probably go back in," I said, unable to read the look on his face. What had he seen?

"Take your temperature tonight," he said, smiling. "Be sure."

"I told you I'm not due for a week."

"You have a bond mate now. He calls." Kee's lips parted, showing perfect white teeth. "Go on, then." He waved me away.

I blinked hard. A warmth stirred behind my eyes, and my head began to ache. I'd never see him again. It was okay; it needed to be this way. But I still felt for a moment as if I could not breathe.

"Live a good life, Kee," I managed to get out.

"You, too."

He got into his car and when the door slammed and the engine started, it was as if the night around me wavered, unreal. I had the thought everything might vanish from one second to the next and I'd be left in a void, alone and lost.

Whispers in my head. My vision edged in fog. A car driving away, my past going along with it.

I needed Alli. *Needed*. With a longing so profound I could barely move forward, my balance off, my head in the stars.

I found my way back to the walkway and up the porch steps. I nearly stumbled through the front door, grabbing the frame to stabilize myself. I automatically closed and locked the front door, then moved unsteadily toward the stairs, waving lights off as I went.

If Oren, Tev and Farrell wanted to return to the living room to watch TV, they'd find their own way back.

Looking up at the stairs, they'd never seemed so vast and daunting. There were so many! I grabbed the banister and pulled my way up, step by step. My palms slipped on the polished wood. Sweat dripped down my back.

But I didn't feel sick. I was fine. Euphoric, actually, because I was headed for Alli. Already, I couldn't wait to take him into my arms. My lover, my Omega, my mate.

Two more steps, and I looked down for a moment to orient myself. The second wave of dizziness passed.

This yearning was strong. It was overtaking my entire body and mind.

When I finally reached the upper landing, silence greeted me. And darkness, save the little light under the window at the end of the hall.

Suddenly, I could no longer sense Alli. I headed for the door to my room, but as I projected ahead of myself, I felt nothing. The room gave off an empty vibe.

I swiveled around, reaching my hand out to the wall to steady the move.

A faint light, almost imperceptible, made a dark orange line underneath the bottom of the door. I approached, put my hand on the knob, and slowly turned it.

If Alli was in the guest room, it had a meaning. But my mind wasn't working. I couldn't understand. Didn't he know he slept with me now?

The door swung open to silent darkness. A single, small lamp lit the far nightstand. A dark shadow, human-shaped, spread across the bed, one leg bent at the knee and slightly turned, arms up, elbows bent, hugging the head, pillowing it.

Alli did not sit up to greet me.

It was actually difficult for me to walk toward him, as if something unseen in the air was blocking me. I stumbled toward the bed.

"Alli? Alli?"

The body on the bed moved slightly. Dark eyes peered at me around a white-sleeved forearm.

I swayed as I stood at the side of the bed. "I think I'm drunk, but we didn't have that much wine, did we?"

"Huh?" His head lifted.

I glanced about. "What are you doing in here?"

He looked away, slowly sitting up. "I can be packed by tomorrow." On the last syllable of that word, his voice cracked.

"What?" I frowned. His words made no sense, and I was suddenly so aroused, so hard for him, my mind was nearly swept away.

"Packed. My stuff." He sniffed and his cheeks shone. He ran his forearms over his eyes.

"Why?"

"I'll be leaving."

"Leaving?" I had no clue how to comprehend that word. But my response sent a weird panic through my veins, that bee sting sensation again, jerking me momentarily to my senses.

"What's wrong, sweetheart?" I asked.

"What's wrong?" Now Alli sat up, crossing his legs and dangling his feet over the side of the bed. "Your lover has returned. The Omega you really want."

I had no sense of my response to that until afterward. After I opened my eyes to see myself on the bed, straddling Alli, my hands on his wrists holding him down, my body pressing fiercely to his all up and down his torso, my hard cock grinding his hip.

My face was inches from his, my breath coming hard, blowing into his wincing face.

Strange growls escaped my throat. I remembered none of the seconds leading up to how I got into this position.

Alli was squirming beneath me. "Let go! Let go!"

His voice seemed desperate, but I could barely hear him. Through our bond, I sensed and saw in my mind's eye, flakes of black ash. I smelled fire. Close. Uncontained.

"Tarin! Ow! Tarin!"

"You're mine," I said. "No one else! You are my Omega. Forever in endless merging. You start the fire and cool the Burn. It is the way." They were sacred words. I had learned them so very long ago, and over the years had convinced myself I'd never have an opportunity to use them.

Alli gasped. "Tarin! Are you in the Burn?"

"No." I pressed hard against Alli, making him gasp. "Not for another five days. Why is everyone asking me this?." I heard myself speak as if from a distance.

"Tarin!" His body stopped squirming. He relaxed beneath me, though his chest still heaved. "Those words. You can't mean—I felt the sting of the bond. I thought it was—collapsing."

"Our bond? It's hotter than ever."

"Yeah. Now I feel it. I—I thought you were going with Kee. I thought--"

"You thought? You dared to close me off?" Why did I sound so furious?

Alli opened his eyes wide and pressed his lips together. "I—didn't. You did. All I felt was a swirl of confusion leading to nothing. It hurt."

My Omega said he hurt. That woke me a little. Was I in the Burn? I couldn't be in the Burn.

A sudden need to care for my Omega nearly overwhelmed me. I opened to him in my mind, all the scents and images and colors that came to me at the thought of him, of his perfect body beneath mine. All my secrets. All my pent up fierce love like a hundred fevers at once, a thousand flames roaring in the voices of all the years, days and minutes of my existence.

I showed him all of this. And more.

Our bed. Our room. Not my room anymore. *Ours.*

A house filled with laughter. The patter of little footfalls and whispering children.

Wrapped around each other, sharing dreams and visions, sharing a future of a hundred Burns, a thousand after a hundred years together, going strong.

Vacationing together in sun and sea; cuddling together by the hearths of a century and a half of winters.

His future gardens, the entire backyard now, all beautifully decorated gardens shivering in the night air.

I could see it all. I wanted all of it and more.

"Tarin, what's happening?" Beneath me, Alli rose up, his arms going around me. "I can see visions. It's beautiful!"

"Do you understand now?"

His eyebrows rose in question.

"You are mine. It's final!"

Tears brightened the corners of his eyes. "And you're my Alpha?"

"Now there is no more question of it."

Through his tears, Alli started laughing. "Tarin, I feel you. All of you. Like flame. I see the heat. I see it."

But it couldn't be. Not yet.

"You're in the Burn," Alli said. "I can feel it. It can't be anything else!"

Then he pulled my head down to him and kissed me, mouth opening, pliant, and I took him with the full force of my kiss, licking past his perfect lips and into his mouth, raising my hands off his wrists and holding his head, my palms on either side of his face.

Alli moaned, and my entire body vibrated with eroticism at that sound.

The bee sting sensations had long vanished. I was comforting my Omega in the instinctive ways of an Alpha in the Burn. Mind. Body. Heart. Soul. Lips. And soon, my cock.

For I could no longer deny it. The fever had come upon me. My Burn was nearly a week early.

# Chapter Seventeen

*Alli*

"Make that sound again," came a whisper in my ear.

After long moments of a kiss so deep I nearly came in my pants, Tarin had his hands on my shirt and was awkwardly unbuttoning it.

I knew what he meant. I moaned in pleasure.

"Yes, that," he said. "I plan on hearing that sound come out of your mouth all night long."

Being near Tarin right now was like being near open flames licking me all over, but Tarin's flame didn't hurt. Tarin's flame drew me into the most aggressive arousal I'd ever experienced.

He batted my hands away as I tried to help him with my shirt. My Alpha was in control and I loved it.

We had both worn nice clothes to dinner. I had on new wool trousers Tarin bought me and had shipped by overnight delivery, along with a new blazer.

Tarin wore one of his suits, no tie, with a shiny, dark blue shirt that brought out the color of his eyes. I loved the blue of his irises behind the drip of dark bangs over his wide, tanned forehead.

As pretty as my clothes were, I wanted them off. Fast.

It was amazing that in his current condition, Tarin could so carefully undo each button until the shirt spread, revealing my chest. I lifted my upper body so I could slide my arms out.

Tarin fell to my chest, kissing it, licking my nipples. A throb ached from my balls to my cock, and pre-cum shot from the tip, a little hot gush, wetting my underwear.

Tarin licked his way down to my belly button, and as he worshipped there, undid my belt and the button, sliding the zipper over my taut and straining flesh.

I lifted my hips and he slid my pants and underwear down all in one shove. I didn't have any shoes on, having kicked them off as I had gotten into the bed, so he pulled the trousers away from my feet and let them drop over the side of the bed.

Freed, my cock popped up, bobbing to my belly but standing up. It wasn't as weighty as Tarin's. And I was young. Pointing toward the ceiling while lying flat on my back was my current talent.

Tarin let out a few inarticulate sounds of pleasure, and began to bite and kiss my thighs. I spread them and he knelt between them, his big hands roaming up and down my legs, making every inch of my skin all over my body prickle in delight. From my toes to the top of my head, from my asshole slicking in readiness to complete our bond to my balls drawn up and churning to let loose with an orgasm, I ached. And it was fantastic.

Tarin drew up a little and nipped, then licked at the head of my cock.

More pre-cum gushed from me, and my balls stirred even more. I could feel the burning of an orgasm starting all over, but especially at the base of my spine and sending electric tingles to my hole.

Tarin sucked the tip of my cock loudly into his mouth.

"Tarin! If you do that I'll come too fast!"

"I intend to make you come over and over again tonight until you are incoherent, until you can't see or hear or breathe and you pass out in my arms," was the reply.

*Oh! Wow!*

Tarin sat up and literally began to tear at his clothes. I watched him yank away his jacket and shirt, then push his trousers down as he was unzipping. I was afraid he had hurt himself, the way he forced the cloth over his erect cock and down his thighs. But he didn't seem hurt in the least.

He crawled over me, fully hard, skin like a desert sun. The intensity between us had me reeling, as if all my thoughts flickered outside my mind instead of safe and secret within.

Tarin ran his palms up and down my chest and sides. "You're mine." Voice like song and sandpaper, rich but gritty with lust. "I am going to prove it to you so you never wonder again where you stand with me."

I loved hearing him reassure me. He made me feel utterly important for the first time in my life. As if I were the center of his world.

Right now, for me, Tarin was everything. I never wanted this night to end.

He had yet to breach me, yet I could already feel him inside and out, surrounding me, holding me, claiming me. Lying back on the bed, I was already making a wet spot from behind.

Tarin's cock batted, thick and strong, at my thighs and hips as he stretched himself over me, settling between my legs. I lifted myself to meet him, wanting to feel his skin against mine all over.

I had taken the classes and read the books on how to present to an Alpha in the Burn. On the stomach, knees bent, thighs spread, rear slightly lifted. Or on the back, legs up, hands on the backs of the thighs to hold the position. Or standing, bent over the side of a bed or couch. A bed was ideal, I remembered reading. The perfect height.

But now I was so lost in sensation and desire, I couldn't think how or what to do first. I wasn't experienced, and what if Tarin didn't like that?

"Tell me what to do," I said.

Tarin shifted a bit to his side, his arm holding his weight off me, his free hand going between my legs, behind my balls, and sliding under my ass, cupping one cheek.

"Just keep being beautiful the way you are."

I clamped down on a wide grin as he leaned in to kiss me deep again, and one of his fingers slid along my crack, circling my slippery hole. It slipped inside me and I gasped against our kiss.

Tarin pulled his mouth back. "Okay?"

*You're in the Burn,* I wanted to say. *How can you keep such control?*

I'd read about the madness for some Alphas who could not control their Burns, how they lost time or passed out or abused Omegas. There was help for them for that, therapy, drugs. But no help for Omegas. We didn't get drugs. We didn't get much beyond simple sex education to deal with our Alpha partners or mates.

But Tarin didn't scare me. He seemed quite sure of himself, yet able to be concerned about me as well. To actually speak to me. To comfort.

"I want more," I replied.

"I can't lie. It will hurt at first. To claim you in this way is my first instinct. But you must be prepared. I won't have it any other way."

He then took his hand away and reached for the bedside drawer. Though it was a guest room, it didn't surprise me he had sex aids nearby. I hadn't snooped. I'd only used one dresser drawer for my own things, and a drawer in the bathroom.

Tarin set some items on the pillow next to my head. Lube. What looked like a thin tube—a vibrator, I guessed. And condoms.

I didn't want any of it. I just wanted him.

I reached awkwardly over my head, smacking the condoms, and said, "Not those."

"When did you last take your prophylactic pill?"

"It's in our food at the farm. So the night before I ran away."

"Those only take a couple days to leave the system," he said.

160

"I know." I lifted my head until my forehead touched his, the heat of him all-encompassing. I wrapped one arm around his naked waist. I saw children in my mind. Our children. The future.

"I want a child by you. So no to protection."

Confusion fogged his eyes. "What?"

It was the wrong moment, in the heat of need, to bring this up, so I let my words tumble out fast and firm.

"I want your child. I want you to seed me. If it doesn't take tonight, we'll try and try until we get it right. I want you. All of you, bare against me, inside me, filling me with your seed. Breed me, Tarin. Make me yours. Fill me with your child."

For a little too long, he remained silent and still. Would this be a deal-breaker? He did want kids, didn't he? I thought about taking my words back, telling him I didn't mean them so early on, before everything was finalized. Before our bond was complete.

Before I could speak, Tarin climbed over me, grabbed me up in a powerful embrace. My head fell back as he kissed me, then he drew his mouth over my neck, licking and biting.

My cock spurted more pre-cum. I wiggled for friction, but he held on tight.

"A child," he said between licks and bites. He went down my body, nipping, kissing, tasting. "A child." He took my cock all the way to the back of his mouth so fast I arched up and came hard.

He milked and drank until there was nothing left. Then he said, "Turn over."

"Yessss!" I scrambled to obey, my cock still hard, still wanting.

And then he was licking me between my cheeks, tongue delving into me. The air on my backside felt cool everywhere except where he touched, and in those places I felt singed.

Tarin let up as I moaned and thrust my ass up, inviting. Now I knew I was in one of the positions I'd learned from books. It felt natural and right.

Tarin's upper body rested against my back. I saw his arm by my head and heard the crackling of the condoms in their wrappers as he gathered them in his big hand and tossed them over the side of the bed.

He grabbed the bottle of lube.

"I don't need it." Pillows muffled my voice.

"You will," he replied. "Because I intend to breed you all night."

"Please! Yes!"

I felt cool liquid down my crack, then deft fingers stroking me. It was so slippery and smooth that again a finger slipped inside me, effortless and welcome. It didn't hurt at all.

Another slipped in, and I felt the stretch. The slight ache. I knew that was nothing compared to the size of Tarin's cock. And then there would be the knot.

A flare of panic rippled through my stomach.

Tarin must have sensed it because he withdrew and his free arm wrapped around my chest, pulling me to him front to back.

"Easy," he whispered in my ear. "We'll take our time."

"I want you," I gasped. "Now."

He chuckled, his hard chest pressing into my back.

I turned slightly. "You're very in control."

He frowned. "I didn't think—that it felt like a regular Burn. And it's too early."

"It is, though, right?"

"I haven't taken my temperature, but yes. You're right. It's come on early. Perhaps awakened by the spontaneous bond."

"That's good, right?"

"As long as we both want this."

"I want this!"

"Just so you know, as the Burn starts, the control is there, and I'm older now, so I handle it well anyway, but as it progresses, I'll be wanting you constantly."

I sighed. "I want you constantly anyway. Now we match."

With my head slightly twisted and his hand supporting it, he kissed me on the corner of my mouth, giving a quick lick.

His fingers never stopped stroking inside me as, for long minutes, he continued to hold me and whisper gently in my ear. He said amazing things, things that sounded perfect and right in the privacy of a bedroom and nowhere else. About how beautiful and tight I was. About my slickness and my every response. Nothing went unnoticed by Tarin concerning me.

My cock was trapped by my body and the bed, hard as ever. It was as if I hadn't come minutes ago. Time meant nothing. I was where I belonged, with purpose and new confidence, in Tarin's arms.

His fingers played inside me, igniting new sensations, finding the sensitive spots of my inner walls that only Omegas possessed.

I groaned over and over into the pillows, raising my hips as my way of begging for more. More Tarin. Specifically, the hot length that teased my thighs and buttocks.

He stretched me, slow and gentle when I really wanted it fast and hard. He used a lot of lube and a lot of patience. It made me feel as if I were coming apart from the inside out.

I couldn't stand it anymore.

"Tarin! Ugh! Put it in me. Please!"

"When I'm ready, sweet."

He had me begging, nearly crying. When his hands slipped out of me and down over my balls, I moved my hips up even more until I was on my knees. I felt like my hole was sucking at the cool air.

"You're gorgeous, Alli. So pretty and open."

Tarin stroked my cock a few times with his other hand, root to tip. It felt like I was gaping for him now, so ready. Too ready.

"Do it, please!" I wiggled my ass.

"How lovely you are." Tarin leaned back and I knew he was looking at me.

My skin flamed all over. As he continued to praise me, the combination of my still-slight embarrassment and extreme arousal had me in near agony. The muscles in my ass contracted.

Tarin hunched over me, his hot body meeting mine, his cock poking between my cheeks. I cried out at the intimate touch.

Then it happened.

The swollen tip pressed my hole. I could feel the blunt pressure. My body instinctively bucked upward, spreading myself as far as I could to take him in.

I pushed back and there was a sort of bursting sensation at my hole for a split-second as he breached the ring and I felt the head slide in.

After that, my muscles took over, sucking him into my channel, welcoming him, making me want to push back hard and have him all now.

"Slow." Tarin's melodic voice washed over me. "My little virgin, you don't want to hurt yourself."

"It doesn't hurt," I managed through gritted teeth.

Tarin pushed in another inch and I felt every slow moment of it, my insides tingling, stretching with a slight ache but nothing more than that.

Everything swelled full and wet back there, throbbing and wonderful, making my whole body taut with desire. To have someone inside me like this for the first time was amazing. I never wanted it to end.

"More." My voice sounded low and rough. "More!"

I moved my ass from left to right.

Tarin swore and I felt another inch.

164

I couldn't wait for him to get to the final stage when he would thrust. I wanted to be fucked. It was a need so great I thought I'd die if I didn't get it. Like I'd been parched my whole life, nothing soothing that thirst until now.

"Tarin! Now!"

I pushed back. Somehow, I'd caught him off guard and I felt his huge cock slide in, stuffing me deeper and deeper until his balls struck my taint. My own cock was so hard it pushed against my belly. I could feel the head wet and dripping.

My forehead dropped to the pillow in a shock of pleasure, though I was still on my knees, butt up. Gods he was big. Almost too big. And he had yet to knot me.

The stretch was odd but only for a few seconds before my muscles got the message that this was good. This was perfect. Omegas were built for mating, and my body wanted it.

My inner passage began to throb hard, and Tarin made a strangled noise of pleasure. "Alli. Oh Alli!"

Slowly, he began to pull out, leaving me both excited with anticipation, and bereft. His cock grazed my inside; the nerves responded with teasing zings in my spine and stomach. In the shaft of my cock.

A white haze began to glaze my mind. I grunted and groaned, wanting him in me all the way again.

Tarin pulled out to the tip and paused, mumbling under his breath as if it was even too much for him. Then he pushed back in and everything went solid white.

My insides convulsed and I nearly screamed, squirming as he impaled me. A deep throb took my breath and I realized I was having my first internal orgasm.

"Alli!" Tarin grabbed me around the waist, pulling him hard to him, holding me through it. "Ah, so good!"

I knew my muscles were milking him now. That was the way we were designed. I orgasmed down there, inside, and the sensation opened me even more to take him, to take his seed. This was breeding.

But more, this was making love, for the bond between us flared with light and sweetness and exultation.

As my orgasm choked me, time went away. Tarin began to thrust just as I wanted and the orgasm kept happening, keeping me in some height of near incomprehensible delight.

He was fucking me good, now, powerful, long thrusts, and my slick made it sound almost filthy but so good. I felt another throb grip Tarin inside me, causing more friction as he pulled out and thrust back in.

Then he was crying out, pumping fast, and my insides were flooded with hot seed as he pulsed. As he came.

"Knot me!" I yelled.

He didn't reply. Probably because he couldn't speak.

My orgasm passed, but pleasure remained as I stilled myself to feel Tarin filling me up with his cock and his semen.

"It's going to happen. I can't stop it," Tarin said in a broken voice.

"Yes! Knot me!" I begged him over and over until the ring of my hole expanded to accommodate a sudden swell of flesh.

The knot was forming at the base of his cock. *Yessss!*

Tarin hugged me hard, holding me tight as I collapsed forward, not quite flat. My ass was still open and lifted for him, but the rest of me lay against the bedspread, my hard cock trapped.

I moaned and groaned as the knot grew, stretching me as it swelled. Now we were locked together, as intimate as it could get.

Tarin began to press light kisses all over my shoulders and neck.

The knot grew inside me so big I thought I'd burst, until finally it began to move. It brushed along my insides, teasing, making me undulate.

166

Tarin said, "Still, baby, still. Gods you're tight. I love it. You're so good. So good for me."

I basked. I could not get enough praise. Raised without much love, I was making up for it now.

It took a long time for the knot to travel the shaft of Tarin's cock. Well, it had a long way to go—he was that big. As we waited, Tarin huffed and gasped the entire time. I felt his spurts inside me, filling me up. He kept coming as the knot worked its way up to the head of his cock where it would finally release the most potent of his seed, then recede.

This was the impregnation process.

If I was ready, my body itself releasing viable eggs in this moment, they would be fertilized. Omegas released more than one egg at a time, which was why we often gave birth to litters of two, three and even four babies at a time.

I wanted it. I wanted babies with Tarin. I wanted everything with him.

Deep inside me, the knot pressed. A surge of liquid gushed forth and I knew that was the moment it released.

Tarin bucked against me, his yell ringing in my ears as his prolonged orgasm culminated in a final crest of ecstasy.

My insides responded by throbbing again, and my second internal orgasm left me breathless, disoriented.

Eventually, Tarin pulled out, releasing me, and I turned in the bed and felt a sudden surge of liquid gush from my gaping hole.

"Stay," Tarin said, motioning toward me. He got up and went into the bathroom, returning with a stack of clean towels.

Immediately, he forced me back and began to clean us up.

His cock bobbed, shiny and still hard. So beautiful, the cut tip almost perfectly round, the ridge flared with continual arousal.

Tarin ran the towel all over my body. The friction of it against my cock made me hiss a bit. He smiled at me and gently stroked it, first with the towel, then his hand.

"Needs to be cleaner," he stated, leaning down and licking it from balls to tip.

He sucked in the head and I came hard, my head smacking back against the pillow.

He was going to do this to me all night? All right, I thought. I'm ready.

Through our bond, his Burn licked me as well, infusing itself into my thoughts, my mental core, my heart.

When I stopped spurting, he lifted up and said to me, "There, all clean again."

We settled into the bed and he wrapped his arms around me until we lay, chest to chest, on our sides.

I think I dozed for a few minutes, but woke immediately when I heard Tarin's breathing increase.

I rolled onto my back and said, "Take me face to face this time."

He looked dreamy, dazed, and pushed my thighs up and apart, this time sliding into me with ease since I was already prepared.

He fucked into me hard and fast until we both came again, yelling, calling each other's names, laughing.

Again and again, we did that all night long.

I lost count of how many times I came, or how many times Tarin knotted me.

I now had a new favorite hobby.

# Chapter Eighteen

*Tarin*

Alli slept in the crook of my arm, the sides of his face tinged pink, eyelashes a smiling, dark brown line against his upper cheeks. His mouth was curved up in dream, sweet, fulfilled, content.

My Burn went on for two full days. There had been some breaks during which I managed to get a robe around my body and make my way to the kitchen for food for us.

Normally, I did not go through my Burns in my own home because of my guests. I was a fairly private person, plus I didn't want to have them feel an ounce of awkwardness around me. I wanted my Omega wards to know they were safe.

But this had been an emergency. I hadn't had time to think, let alone plan any sort of getaway.

Alli woke, his eyelids fluttering, and turned to press his naked body tighter against me. One of his legs was thrown over mine. The covers went up to our legs only. The rest of his lovely body was revealed to me, from that sweet, plush ass to his flat hairless chest, to the luscious cock, soft now, that nestled against my hip.

It had been his first time, and he'd been amazing. The most amazing lover I'd ever had.

Alli squeezed his arm around my waist and lifted his head, balancing on his elbow and looking down at me.

I raised my eyebrows, my smile turning to a grin. That look on his face, it made me want to give him the world.

"I have questions," he said, licking his lips, finding his morning voice.

"Yes?"

He winced a little. "Not to spoil the mood, but--"

"But what?"

"Tarin, tell me about Kee. I thought—I thought--"

I put a gentle finger to my lips. "Shh. No need to ever worry about him again, my love."

The way he blinked those lashes at me. My cock swelled again. Soon. Soon I would be pummeling him with my own big knot again. And again. Both in and out of the Burn.

I wanted him all the time now.

I knew I would never get enough.

"But you and he--" Alli began.

"Kee is bonded to another Alpha now," I said softly, my fingers drawing up over his cheek to weave into the dark hair on the side of his head. "He wanted privacy to tell me because he thought I wouldn't take it well, that I'd be hurt. A week ago, I would have. When I met you, my heart was already broken. That's why I couldn't allow myself to believe in our instant rapport. But now I had my own bonding story to tell him in return. Do you understand now?"

His eyebrows came together. "You told him about me?"

"Of course I did. You are the center of my life now. I want the entire world to know."

"You do?"

"I do." I flipped him over and lay between his legs, keeping most of my weight on my knees. "I want to celebrate. I want to shout it from rooftops, mountain tops, the very clouds themselves."

"I didn't know you were soooo romantic," Alli said, mouth twisting. Then he burst out, "How did I get so lucky?"

Ah, but it was I who was the lucky one.

I leaned down and kissed him hard. When his arms came around my neck to pull me closer, I reveled in it.

I had finally found my true family.

# Epilogue

Alli was hornier than ever, even with his swollen belly.

I ran my hands up and down the hill of it, feeling the smooth skin and the swell of the babies within. Three of them.

My other hand played with his cock. He said it made him feel more relaxed with the contractions if I made him come.

That was no hardship.

He still had hours before he would be ready to go to the hospital. They said to have him rest in his own bed until the contractions went to five minutes apart.

This gave us privacy so I could assist Alli through the pain.

He was more beautiful than ever pregnant, his skin glowing, his eyes soft and often unfocused, the happiness he felt pouring through our bond.

Lying naked on his back on the bed, knees bent, legs spread, he was the most gorgeous being I'd ever seen. I could not get my fill of him.

I massaged his balls. I fingered his hole. I sucked his cock as contractions came and went. Sucking him when they started to wave over him, making him tense in pain, calmed him, helped distract him.

He'd already come twice in my hand, panting.

"I love you," he gasped. Then tears threatened to spill and I took him in my arms and soothed him.

"Are you afraid, sweet?" I asked.

"A little."

"You'll do fine. And I will be at your side every moment."

"Tarin, our babies are finally coming."

"I know. It's a beautiful day for a triple birthday."

"Is it? Is it perfect?" he asked.

"Perfect."

"Good."

I covered him with a light sheet and he napped in my arms.

When it came time to go to the hospital, he trembled as I supported him down the steps and into the garage.

At the hospital, he was given a gown that opened in the back. With the eagerness of youth and the never-ceasing love we both projected back and forth through our bond, he gave birth to three healthy boys, two Alphas and an Omega.

I couldn't believe it. I was the father of three sons now. We were fathers. Their little scrunched faces and little wrinkled hands and feet were the most beautiful things I'd ever seen, with the exception of my bond mate.

I held all three boys in my arms and against my chest, leaning slightly to show Alli what we had made.

"Look," I said. "The perfect number to juggle."

"You're *not* juggling our babies," he said with a snarl.

I laughed. "We'll see."

The next day when we arrived home—our family expanded to five now—my wards met us at the door.

Everyone wanted to hold the babies. To coo and smile at them. To play with them.

From the tops of the trees, in the wind, from the clouds themselves I wanted to announce their arrival to the world. Three beautiful boys made of light and dream, made of our fated love.

Alli and I. We were one now.

Whether destined or not, it didn't matter. Our love was real. Our lives forever changed because of one momentary meeting on a dark and littered street on a night when a very hungry and handsome boy followed an instinct that led him to his true home.

THE END

Dear Reader:

Thank you for reading *Omega Chattel*: *The Omega Misfits Book 5.*

I had been wanting to write about an Omega runaway ever since I started this series. Now I got my chance and it was an amazing experience.

Next on my agenda is book 6 in *The Omega Misfits* series, **Omega Untamed.** This will be Kee's story. While writing **Omega Chattel,** I was unsure if I was going to have the missing Omega Kee show up in the end or not. Part of me thought, "Maybe he's been killed and Tarin will have to go through that." But when I discussed it with my friend and talented fellow author Jackie North, she emphatically told me Kee must have his own story and he cannot die! So you have her to thank for saving Kee's life. Not only that, as soon as we talked, Kee's story began to unfold in my mind and I'm hard at work on it.

The link for Kee's story, **Omega Untamed**, is already up! It's a pre-order until September 15, 2020, and if you're reading this after that date, then it is already live.

## mybook.to/omegauntamed

I hope you continue to stay along with me on this journey where I continue my discovery of this wonderful omegaverse genre with many more Omega Misfits books to come!

Happy Reading!

Love, Wendy Rathbone

# About Wendy Rathbone

*Read Wendy Rathbone… where imposters and outcasts, princes and lost boys always find their happily every after.*

I have written in all genres: sci-fi, fantasy, horror, paranormal, contemporary, erotica, romance. But I keep coming back to romance as the main focus. Gay romance. Male/male romance. The idea of two men falling in love is irresistible to me. It's all I write now.

All my books are available on Amazon and most are in Kindle Unlimited. So if you have the urge, go take a look. See what's on the shelf.

Male/male romance books by Wendy:

**The Kingdom of Slaves Series**
(contemporary fantasy mm romance)

The Slave Palace
The Slave Harem
Master of Halloween (short story)

**The Omega Misfits** (Omegaverse mm romance)

Trust No Alpha
The Alpha's Fake Mate
Alpha's Embrace
Single Omega Dad
Omega Chattel
Omega Untamed (coming Sept. 15)

**The Imposter Series** (fantasy mm romance)

The Imposter Prince
The Imposter King

**The Moonling Prince Series** (fantasy, sci fi mm romance)

The Moonling Prince
The Coming of the Light

**The Foundling Series** (contemporary billionaire mm romance trilogy)

Rescue Me
Sacrifice Me
Remember Me

**The Fantastic Immortals Series** (fantasy/myth mm romance)

Ganymede: Abducted by the Gods
Zeus: Conquering his Heart

**Stand Alone Novels**

*Sci Fi MM Romance*

Solstice Gift (holiday)
Not Another Hero
Cocky Virgin Prince
Prey
Scoundrel
The Android and the Thief
Letters to an Android

*Fantasy MM Romance*

Lord Vampyre
Lace
Snow of the White Hills (mm fairy tale)
The Elves of Christmas (holiday fantasy mm romance)

*Contemporary MM Romance*

Romantically Incorrect
Snowfall and Romance (Christmas novel)
The Bodyguard's Valentine
Buying You

**Contact links for Wendy Rathbone:**

Join my Facebook group Wendyland. I post updates, cover reveals, snippets, sales and other fun stuff every day: https://www.facebook.com/groups/718074255203918/

Friend me on Facebook: https://www.facebook.com/wendy.rathbone.3

Follow my Amazon author page: https://www.amazon.com/Wendy-Rathbone/e/B00B0O9BMS/ref=dp_byline_cont_ebooks_1

Follow me on Bookbub: https://www.bookbub.com/authors/wendy-rathbone

## OMEGA UNTAMED
## The Omega Misfits Book 6
## Wendy Rathbone

Kee is a beautiful Omega and popular rent boy living in a part of Old Town called the Trenches. He's also an untamable addict. Wild and troubled, Kee is kidnapped by Alpha drug lords who think he knows too much.

Trapped, Kee longs for a way out of the hole he's dug for himself...but who would rescue a crazy Omega sex worker?

One Alpha will. His name is Bast. Bast knows he can't tame Kee through kindness, but he still wants him for his very own.

Kee needs an Alpha who will take control, hold him down, keep him from the worst of himself. Turns out, Bast is the very man for the job.

Non-shifter omegaverse, mpreg, rescue, an uninhibited Omega, a tough Alpha with a heart of gold, daddy care, bonding/knotting and HEA.

## SINGLE OMEGA DAD
## The Omega Misfits Book 4
## Wendy Rathbone

My new financial guardian, Mathias, is a cold, self-centered, rude-ass Alpha and the son of one of the wealthiest men in the country. To him, I am a burden on society, only fit to live on a chattel farm.

It doesn't matter that I'm drawn to him, to his ominous presence and chiseled jaw, his muscular body in his fitted silk suits. I'm a single dad with kids and responsibilities --I don't have time for that rich bastard.

He keeps coming by the house so I can sign documents, fine. But then he's got cute gifts for my kids.

It's got to stop. I don't have time to fix him. Don't have time to fall in love with an Alpha right now.

A non-shifter Alpha/Omega love story with mpreg, a single widower Omega dad, an Alpha who cannot knot, emotional issues, two adorable identical twin boys, and an HEA.

Some characters from "Trust No Alpha" make appearances in this novel, however, this book is a standalone read.

## TRUST NO ALPHA
## The Omega Misfits, Book 1
## Wendy Rathbone

It's a world gone mad. The Alphas are out of control. When you discover you're not who you thought you were, the nightmare begins.

KRIS
At age eighteen, life as he knows it is over for Kris. A secret to his nature he was not aware of has been revealed.

Now, kept as a prisoner in a locked room in the mansion of his wealthy father, Kris is at the mercy of Alpha laws and Alpha domination.

Things take a turn for the worse when his own litter mate threatens him, and his father starts behaving strangely around him.

Escape is his only hope. But where can he go in a world that allows him no rights?

THORNE
Marked as a dangerous Alpha, and living a secluded life alone and unloved, Thorne still grieves for the mate whose death he feels responsible for.

Years have passed, and he refuses to even try to function in normal society.

One day he discovers a young man on his property, disheveled, desperate, and scared. He acts like a runaway Omega, but he doesn't smell like one.

What is this boy? And why does Thorne feel an immediate need to protect him? To bond him? To make him his?

A non-shifter, Omegaverse love story of rescue, first time, fertility issues and an HEA. Standalone read. 65,500 words. (While Omegas are birth-fathers in this universe, there is no on-page mpreg in this book.)

## THE ALPHA'S FAKE MATE
### The Omega Misfits, Book 2
### Wendy Rathbone

The Alphas think they own everything. Including people. Well, I'm here to say they don't own me, and I will never let one of those bastards touch me again.

The frenzy of their Burn cannot be trusted. I know from experience. My first time with an Alpha nearly ended in my death. And because of the laws which favor Alpha rights, and place a large number of unbonded, adult Omegas on chattel farms, my abuser can never be tried for his crimes against me.

Omegas are being hurt. Omegas are dying.

All Alphas are violent. Or so I believe. Until I meet Orion.

Ori is everything a guy could want in a mate. Six foot three. Beautiful brown wavy hair. Bright, dark eyes. Muscles like chiseled marble. He even says "please" and "thank you" at all the right times. He's got it all, except he's an Alpha.

Though he has given me a room in his home free of charge, and has signed fake paperwork saying we are bonded so I don't have to answer my attacker's claim, can I trust him?

But now I'm in danger. If I don't take a real mate, my life as I know it will be over. Can I believe in the goodness of Ori? Can I learn to love again?

A non-shifter, fake mate, Alpha/Omega love story. Rescue. First time. Omegaverse. Mpreg. Healing from sexual trauma. (All books in The Omega Misfits series are standalone reads and can be read in any order.) 61k words.

### ALPHA'S EMBRACE
### The Omega Misfits, Book 3
### Wendy Rathbone

I am Misha. My name was given to me at birth by the doctor who delivered me. I have never known my parents. I live in a ten by ten space with one window, a sink and toilet, a bed and a locked door. Once a day I'm taken to an outdoor exercise area. I am allowed a limited access tablet and tutored online by computer programs. I have one friend I talk to through a tiny crack in the wall. His name is Cedric and he has trouble keeping himself quiet. When he isn't talking to me about monsters and demons, he screams all the time.

Why is my life so isolated and depressing? Because I am a Sylph. Sylphs are the byproduct of illegal Omega to Omega matings. We are all beautiful, but 99.9% are born insane. The rarest of Sylphs, like me, show no outward signs of madness or brain damage, but we live in institutions because we cannot be trusted.

All of us Sylphs who have lived long enough to pass through puberty have hypersexual disorder which makes life even more difficult for us, let alone our keepers. It is like something Alphas call the Burn, a mating urge Alphas experience once every couple of months.

But we're Sylphs, not Alphas, and this Burn thing? We experience it all the time. It's a huge problem and why we are kept isolated. Most of us don't survive through our teens because of it.

One day, a handsome Alpha comes to interview and study me. He calls himself the Chief of Staff but his real name is Geo. Like magic, I fall in love with him instantly. I do everything I can to seduce him. He will have none of it because touch between an Alpha and a Sylph is taboo. But I have plans. No matter what, I intend to bond him and make him mine. Forever.

A non-shifter Alpha/Omega-Sylph love story of forbidden love, rescue, and HEA. Standalone read. No Mpreg. 58k words

## THE SLAVE PALACE
Wulf and Locke
WENDY RATHBONE

Conquered. Captured. Sold as a pleasure slave.

After being taken as a prisoner of war, Wulf fights his captors and is sold as a One-Night Thrall to be used and abused, then put to death. He is purchased by a high ranking master of the famous Slave Palace. Why Locke buys him, Wulf has no clue, but something about this master is intriguing. Instead of abuse, Wulf is plied with luxuries he has never known by a man who actually seems to respect him.

Jaded. Looking for a challenge.

Eminent Master Locke takes on a bet with his best friend that he can't train and tame a dangerous One-Night Thrall in ten days. But something about this slave stirs him like no other before. All bets aside, Locke has the urge to keep Wulf, as well as save his life. But Wulf is fierce, unwilling, and his consent papers have been forged. If Wulf doesn't soon submit to his role as a slave, he will be sent to death as a prisoner of war.

A sweet, slow-burn love story taking place on an alternate contemporary Earth where owning pleasure slaves is legal.

## LORD VAMPYRE
### Wendy Rathbone

When Lord Neverelle becomes a guest at Cliffside Keep, Vanni watches helplessly as Damion, the young man he's grown up with and secretly loves, falls for the alluring and seductive stranger. Lord Neverelle is danger incarnate, and soon takes control of the household.

Not satisfied with Damion alone, Never uses a vampire trick called "the tempt" to compel Vanni, who is swept into a love triangle that includes fiery passion and nightly threesomes.

Now Vanni must ask himself, is any of this consensual? And what about Damion—does he really want to be with Vanni, or is it all a sensual play controlled by vampire compulsion?

M/M and M/M/M romance.

## The Imposter Prince
### Book 1 in The Imposter Series
### Wendy Rathbone

***His love for an enemy prince threatens his very life.***

Dare does not mind serving the spoiled and cruel Prince Darius. Growing up with him, Dare does everything for Darius including homework, bed play demands, and even doubling for him as the prince grows too paranoid to face even the smallest of crowds.

But everything changes in a single moment when Dare, while posing as Darius, is abducted by the enemy.

A captive in a new and hostile land, Dare meets another prince who seems just as indulged and rotten as Darius—until Dare gets to know him, until they fall in love. Against his will, Dare must continue to play the role of Prince Darius for real, or risk everything: his love, his land, and his very life.

His only chance for survival is to keep a secret from the one he loves, a secret that is also killing him.

A male/male, enemies to lovers novel of mad kings, troubled princes, abduction, fevers, cold dungeons, warm hearths, comfort, wine, and true love.

## BUYING YOU
### Wendy Rathbone

It's one thing to be a beautiful cover model on billboards, buses and magazine covers. It's quite another to be sold as one.

Prized for his looks, Dane knows it's shallow, but he is on his way to having it all. It feels good to be gorgeous, smart and have top designers from around the world requesting him.

When he returns to his hometown to participate in a small Date-For-Charity auction, it seems harmless enough—until a hooded man walks in and bids higher on him than anyone else. Dane is intrigued but nervous when he finds out the guy has vanished after the winning bid, leaving only a limo behind to whisk Dane off into the night.

Enemies to lovers, opposites attract, and hot steamy nights that challenge two guys' trust issues along with their biggest fears.

## SONS OF NEVERLAND
### *A Deliciously Dark Male/Male Romance*
## <u>Della Van Hise</u>

Set against a backdrop of contemporary culture, *Sons of Neverland* explores the universal questions of love, sex and death - the three most crucial challenges every human being must face. Stefan London is a grieving man, suffering the loss of his young daughter. When he goes to a science fiction convention in the hopes of meeting her friends, he encounters instead a man who is dangerously seductive. Lured into the night, Stefan soon discovers himself in a world where vampires are real, and immortality is only a kiss away.

But the price of eternal life is high, and as his handsome maker warns, "Through my blood you will learn a secret that will compel you to live forever, yet a secret so sinister it will haunt you for that same eternity."

The secret will haunt you, too.

———

*A deliciously dark male/male romance. First time, enemies to lovers, love/hate relationship, HEA.*

## YEAR OF THE RAM
### Della Van Hise

Only after Star Commander Morgan Diego becomes an exile as a result of a Galaxy Corps political blunder does he begin to realize how much he valued the companionship of his second in command - the mysterious Lucien, an Alfarian who is more elfen than human, with peculiar powers & abilities which begin to unfold as he, too, realizes what he has lost.

Separated by circumstance from his former life, Morgan is thrust into a world where he must survive by his wits. When he meets a peculiar little old man calling himself Kim Le, Morgan finds himself in a situation where he is required to master The Art - not only a form of human & extraterrestrial martial arts, but a way of living that will alter his life forever.

At the temple, he is introduced to his new teacher, another Alfarian man who begins to steal his heart - a heart which is already promised to Lucien. Torn and conflicted, Morgan struggles with the world he left behind and the world he now inhabits.

Beginning to believe he may never again return to his ship and to the friends and loved ones he left behind, he is all the more frustrated and heartbroken when a new Master arrives at the temple: a man to whom Morgan is immediately drawn both mentally and physically, a man who is strikingly familiar... yet utterly alien.

**Eye Scry Publications**
**www.eyescrypublications.com**

www.ingramcontent.com/pod-product-compliance
Lightning Source LLC
Chambersburg PA
CBHW020610250626
47154CB00004B/1444